The North K
holding Bald
building—if t
was still alive

From his vantage point in a line of cars parked on the street, the Executioner considered the problem. Any attempt to raid the building would cause the North Koreans to either flee or, worse, kill Baldero and cut their losses before they escaped. That could not be permitted. A surgical strike was called for—and the time for action had arrived.

Bolan made sure his weapons were secure in their holsters and that he carried a full complement of spare magazines, drawing from the last of the stores in his war bag. Then he screwed the custom-built suppressor to the threaded barrel of his Beretta 93-R, held the pistol low against his leg and walked up to the front of the curio shop.

Knowing that at any moment, a shotgun blast could chop him in half at the waist, Bolan took a step back and planted a combat-booted foot on the wooden door. It splintered and slammed inward, reverberating off the wall inside.

Bolan dived into the room.

Rescue was coming—and with it, hell.

MACK BOLAN®
The Executioner

#311 Night of the Knives
#312 Death Gamble
#313 Lockdown
#314 Lethal Payload
#315 Agent of Peril
#316 Poison Justice
#317 Hour of Judgment
#318 Code of Resistance
#319 Entry Point
#320 Exit Code
#321 Suicide Highway
#322 Time Bomb
#323 Soft Target
#324 Terminal Zone
#325 Edge of Hell
#326 Blood Tide
#327 Serpent's Lair
#328 Triangle of Terror
#329 Hostile Crossing
#330 Dual Action
#331 Assault Force
#332 Slaughter House
#333 Aftershock
#334 Jungle Justice
#335 Blood Vector
#336 Homeland Terror
#337 Tropic Blast
#338 Nuclear Reaction
#339 Deadly Contact
#340 Splinter Cell
#341 Rebel Force
#342 Double Play
#343 Border War
#344 Primal Law
#345 Orange Alert
#346 Vigilante Run
#347 Dragon's Den
#348 Carnage Code
#349 Firestorm
#350 Volatile Agent
#351 Hell Night
#352 Killing Trade
#353 Black Death Reprise
#354 Ambush Force
#355 Outback Assault
#356 Defense Breach
#357 Extreme Justice
#358 Blood Toll
#359 Desperate Passage
#360 Mission to Burma
#361 Final Resort
#362 Patriot Acts
#363 Face of Terror
#364 Hostile Odds
#365 Collision Course
#366 Pele's Fire
#367 Loose Cannon
#368 Crisis Nation
#369 Dangerous Tides
#370 Dark Alliance
#371 Fire Zone
#372 Lethal Compound
#373 Code of Honor
#374 System Corruption
#375 Salvador Strike
#376 Frontier Fury
#377 Desperate Cargo
#378 Death Run
#379 Deep Recon
#380 Silent Threat
#381 Killing Ground
#382 Threat Factor
#383 Raw Fury
#384 Cartel Clash
#385 Recovery Force
#386 Crucial Intercept

The Don Pendleton's

Executioner®

CRUCIAL INTERCEPT

TORONTO • NEW YORK • LONDON
AMSTERDAM • PARIS • SYDNEY • HAMBURG
STOCKHOLM • ATHENS • TOKYO • MILAN
MADRID • WARSAW • BUDAPEST • AUCKLAND

Recycling programs
for this product may
not exist in your area.

First edition January 2011

ISBN-13: 978-0-373-64386-8

Special thanks and acknowledgment to
Phil Elmore for his contribution to this work.

CRUCIAL INTERCEPT

Printed in U.S.A.

The best weapon against an enemy is another enemy.

—Friedrich Nietzsche
1844–1900

Terrorism will not be tolerated in the suburban backyards and city streets of America—not on my watch. I will attack from all sides, from every angle, until the enemies inevitably turn their guns on each other.

—Mack Bolan

THE MACK BOLAN LEGEND

Nothing less than a war could have fashioned the destiny of the man called Mack Bolan. Bolan earned the Executioner title in the jungle hell of Vietnam.

But this soldier also wore another name—Sergeant Mercy. He was so tagged because of the compassion he showed to wounded comrades-in-arms and Vietnamese civilians.

Mack Bolan's second tour of duty ended prematurely when he was given emergency leave to return home and bury his family, victims of the Mob. Then he declared a one-man war against the Mafia.

He confronted the Families head-on from coast to coast, and soon a hope of victory began to appear. But Bolan had broken society's every rule. That same society started gunning for this elusive warrior—to no avail.

So Bolan was offered amnesty to work within the system against terrorism. This time, as an employee of Uncle Sam, Bolan became Colonel John Phoenix. With a command center at Stony Man Farm in Virginia, he and his new allies—Able Team and Phoenix Force—waged relentless war on a new adversary: the KGB.

But when his one true love, April Rose, died at the hands of the Soviet terror machine, Bolan severed all ties with Establishment authority.

Now, after a lengthy lone-wolf struggle and much soul-searching, the Executioner has agreed to enter an "arm's-length" alliance with his government once more, reserving the right to pursue personal missions in his Everlasting War.

Mack Bolan pulled the Crown Victoria sedan into the only free slot among the convenience store's gas pumps, jockeying for position among the other drivers already fueling up. The man still known to some as the Executioner was just outside Williamsburg, Virginia, having spent the past several hours burning up state highways. The Crown Victoria, an FOUO—for official use only—vehicle on loan from a CIA motor pool, was a "plainclothes" interceptor model. Its big up-rated 250 horsepower V8 engine drove seventeen-inch stamped steel wheels wearing 235/55/17 high-performance rubber, all of it held together by a heavy-duty suspension and frame. The powerful car had served Bolan well, bearing him swiftly from Langley to Charlottesville, then to Lynchburg, and finally to Richmond, where he'd received the call from the Farm that sent him tearing up the road to Williamsburg.

Bolan snapped open his secure satellite phone and dialed the number that would, through a circuitous and redundantly encrypted route, connect him with Stony Man Farm in Virginia. The nerve center for the Sensitive Operations Group, a covert arm of the United States Justice Department, had been the scene of furious activity overnight.

Bolan had gotten no more sleep than had the cyber team at the Farm, for while they traced his location, coordinated with local law enforcement, and fed new destinations to the Executioner, he had pushed the Crown Victoria to reach each and every one of the target zones. Each time, they had been one step behind their quarry. The soldier understood from long experience that sometimes you had to hurry up and wait. There was little he could do but chase down the leads passed on to him by the Farm. Eventually, his path would intercept those of the person or persons he sought, likely with violent results.

He would see to that.

The first urgent contact from the Farm had come just before midnight. Bolan had been staying in a motel near Langley, taking some long-overdue down time to rest after his latest debriefing trip to Wonderland and a meet with Hal Brognola. While he maintained an arm's length relationship with the United States government's covert counterterrorism network, Brognola transcended any bureaucratic boundaries or barriers. He liked to keep the big Fed informed of what he learned, each and every time he stepped onto the latest battlefield in his endless war against terror and injustice. The cyber team at the Farm could use the intel to update—or close—files on various threats.

The call alone, when it woke him, would have been enough to leave him instantly alert—but the words of Barbara Price, Stony Man's mission controller, had left no doubt.

"Striker," Price had said, using the Farm's code name for the Executioner, "somebody's shooting up Virginia."

Bolan had switched on the large color television, after finding the oversized motel remote on top of the set. Predictably, every one of the cable news channels and at least two local Virginia television stations were all over the story. A series of high-profile shootings, committed by groups of men wielding automatic weapons, had torn up several public locations in Charlottesville. The first, in the early evening, had ripped apart an Internet café just off the campus of the University of Virginia, which had sparked fears of another Virginia Tech–style massacre. Nobody had been killed, but significant damage to the facility had been done.

Less than an hour after the computer lab shooting, another one-sided gun battle had shot up a public Laundromat in downtown Charlottesville. Then, an hour and a half after that, a convenience store on the outskirts of the city had taken a broadside from what one witness described as "four Chinese men with Uzis." This was the worst of the incidents, to that point; a clerk working behind the front counter had been tagged by a bullet. The young man had died on the way to the hospital.

It was the report of "four Chinese men" with automatic weapons that worried the men and women at the Farm, and it was this concern—as well as the shootings occurring in close succession in a major metropolitan area—that had tripped warning flags. There were no current reports of new terrorist threats from Asian fringe groups, Asian gangs, or even from within elements of nominally hostile governments such as China. Bolan's jaw had tightened, at that. It had not been so long ago that he had found himself dealing with heavily armed and very hostile Chinese sleeper cells on American soil in Hawaii. The Chinese government had dismissed the attacks as the work of rogue elements in their military. A lot of people had died before it was over, and Bolan had no desire to see a repeat performance from yet another highly organized and disciplined gathering of "rogue" operatives trained and equipped in Communist China.

When he had said as much, Price had dismissed it as unlikely. Aaron "the Bear" Kurtzman, Stony Man's computer expert and the leader of the Farm's cyber team, had found no indication of a coordinated terror effort. There was no communications traffic or Internet traffic to indicate it, and very little in the way of official government maneuvering. At least, there was nothing to which the Farm's team could traçe the violence. That was enough to satisfy Bolan on that score, at least for now, but it did leave the question of what *was* happening in Virginia—and he had said as much.

"That," Price had replied over the secure line, "we think we do know, at least in part. Bear and his people have been burning up the ether trying to get what surveillance data there was to be had. We've managed to extract security camera images from two locations. The first is from the Internet café, and the second is from the convenience store. Using image enhancement technology on the convenience store video footage, we've compared it to a fairly clear picture from the Web cameras in the computer lab. There's a link, which I'm sending to your phone now."

Bolan had taken his phone from his ear to see the data transfer icon blinking. It did not take long for the image to load on his own small color screen. The picture itself was black-and-white, bearing the unmistakable pixel dithering of an image that has been put through the digital wringer to make it more clear. It was the face of a man with long, dark hair.

"Who's this?" Bolan asked, putting the phone back to his ear.

"That," Price said, "is Daniel Baldero. Thirty-years-old. Five-foot-ten, 270 pounds. Paid for college by joining the Air Force. Honorable discharge. Earned a couple of degrees in computer programming before he was finished going to school, in Newport News. Last address of record, according to the Virginia DMV, is Charlottesville, Virginia. Mr. Baldero can be, thanks to the footage we've used to identify him, positively placed at the scene of two out of three of those shootings."

"Doing what?"

"Running for his life, from what we can see," Price said.

"So he's not one of the shooters."

"No," Price said. "And of course we can't place him at the laundry shooting because there were no functioning cameras there. But as coincidences go—"

"It's a pretty big one," Bolan agreed. "This Baldero is either the unluckiest man in Virginia, or something's fishy and he's involved."

"It gets more interesting," Price said. "Mr. Baldero is a computer programmer and cryptographer by trade, formerly employed by the Central Intelligence Agency."

"Formerly," Bolan repeated.

"As of two weeks ago," Price reported. "He resigned without explanation."

"Is he on the run?"

"We checked, and they deny it," Price had said. "Logically, there's no reason he *should* be on the run, at least not from the CIA. They have no reason to chase him down. He's just a former employee, as far as they're concerned, and not one with any sort of contract to which they could hold him."

"But again, as coincidences go," Bolan said.

"It's a pretty big one," Price echoed. "The Man wants us on this, Striker, and Hal's given us the green light."

"I'll leave immediately," Bolan said. "But I'm going to need transportation. The rental I'm driving hasn't got the guts for a field operation."

"We've got a car on its way to you by courier," Price said. "Hal's made an arrangement with the CIA. You'll get one from their motor pool."

"There's that word again." Bolan frowned at the phone. "I'm going to need weapons and equipment for an extended field operation."

"Already in the car and on the way to your door," Price said. "Cowboy keeps a few specially prepared care packages ready and waiting for little emergencies like these." John "Cowboy" Kissinger was the Farm's armorer. He had personally tuned the Beretta 93-R machine pistol in the leather shoulder holster Bolan was strapping on, and he had custom-built the suppressor fitted to the weapon. He had also done an accuracy job on the .44 Magnum Desert Eagle that was Bolan's other nearly constant companion, which he carried in a Kydex holster in his waistband on his right hip.

"Then I'm not going to waste any more time talking," Bolan said, watching headlights pan across the curtains of the motel room's window. "Unless it's another coincidence, the car is just arriving. Your timing is impeccable."

"We try," Price said. "Oh, and be sure to check inside the trunk." When she spoke again, her tone was warmer, but also more anxious. "Be careful, Striker."

"Always, Barb."

"Good hunting."

"Thanks. Striker out." He closed the phone.

The courier was at the door just as Bolan opened it—the man said not a word. He was dressed in slacks and a blazer and had about him what Bolan thought of as the "junior G-man" look. He nodded and tossed the keys to Bolan, which were for the Crown Victoria now idling in front of Bolan's open motel-room door. Then he disappeared around the corner of the building.

Bolan looked at the car, then back to where the courier had been. He shook his head slightly.

There was work to do.

THAT PHONE CALL had been one long, tiring drive ago on only half a night's sleep, fueled by truck-stop coffee and a fast-food breakfast consumed at highway speed. Since then, the Executioner had tracked the increasingly violent outbreaks of gunfire from site to site in Virginia. The Farm relayed to him the location each time it happened, but Bolan knew as well as Price did that they would not get ahead of the shooters by playing a reactive game. They needed to get in front of the gunners, whoever they were.

He had checked each site, the latest a motel in Williamsburg that had been blown half to hell. Yet again, there was no evidence of the shooters themselves. He had phoned in and reported as much. Price had promised that the follow-up field team, a covert Justice analysis unit protected by blacksuit gunners from Stony Man, would check for evidence he might have missed in his cursory inspection, as they had been doing behind him all night. They would also see if there were any local surveillance sources to be pulled for analysis. That didn't concern Bolan, at least not immediately. He would be surprised if the tapes showed anything of use except to confirm Baldero's presence. Intelligence on the shooters would be helpful, but even that wasn't crucial at the moment. The only thing that mattered was getting out in front of the shooters, and that depended on the pattern analysis Stony Man had been working on.

"Price here."

"Striker," Bolan said. "Same story here."

"You're still outside Williamsburg?"

"Yes," he said. "Your crew can move in on the motel. I saw a lot of shell casings but not much else. No sign of our boy, and nothing of use. Barb, you've got to get me in front of this. Has Bear run his pattern analysis?"

"Got you right here, Striker." Aaron Kurtzman's voice came over the line. "I'm here with Barb. Our instincts have been right all along. We're plotting the shootings and they make a line, more or less. That puts the next possible cluster of targets in a more or less straight line through Hampton, Newport News and Norfolk, if the pattern holds."

"Then I'm headed to—" Bolan began. He stopped.

"Striker?" Price asked in Bolan's ear. The soldier's head snapped left, then right. His eyes narrowed.

"I hear gunshots," Bolan said. He snapped the phone shut

and half-vaulted the hood of the Crown Victoria, throwing himself behind the wheel and slamming the door shut. The big tires squealed and the engine roared as he floored the vehicle, tearing out of the convenience store parking lot. Horns honked as he cut off several vehicles. The car whipped onto the highway and he hit the automatic windows, rolling them all the way down on both sides, fore and aft.

He heard it again, then—the unmistakable sound of automatic gunfire in the distance, moving away from him. He pushed the interceptor onward, yanking the wheel hard left, cutting across a side street and taking another.

When he heard the next burst of shots, it was louder. He was getting closer. He scanned the traffic far ahead of him.

Logistically, this was very bad. It was broad daylight. A running gun battle in an American city, especially an American *tourist* city, was going to pour gasoline on the already raging media fire over the cluster of shootings throughout the night. The Executioner had been listening to news-talk radio throughout his nighttime chase. Every station was bubbling over with sensational reporting on the "terrorist attacks," with hysterical talking heads manning their desks and filling the airwaves with commentary from "experts." The incessant speculation and mindless chatter had eventually become so much background noise to Bolan, who understood only too well the reality that the reporters were playing at analyzing.

From a pocket of his blacksuit—the formfitting black combat clothing that could pass for casual street clothes to the untrained eye, especially when worn under a light windbreaker as he was doing—Bolan removed a tiny earbud headset and donned it. He flipped open his secure sat phone and replaced the device in his pocket after hitting the first speed dial. Price's voice came to him almost instantly, filtered through the earpiece.

"Striker?"

"I'm in pursuit, target or targets unknown." He consulted

the GPS unit on his dashboard and read off the coordinates and heading. As he did so, he heard more gunfire and thought he could make out muzzle flashes in the distance. It was hard to tell in the daylight. "Tracking gunfire specifically. To guess, I'd say our shooters weren't quite done with Williamsburg."

"You're across town from the motel they hit," Price said, though Bolan was perfectly aware of his position. "If you stay on this heading, you'll end up hitting Norfolk, more or less."

"Kudos to Bear, then," Bolan said. "Barb, I have a theory."

"Striker?"

"Our boy Baldero. He's rabbiting. Think about it. If you were suddenly a fugitive, if someone or some group of someones was trying to shoot you, where would you go? A computer lab, to try and contact help. Baldero's a tech geek, right? That's familiar. That's where he'd head. Motels, convenience stores, Laundromats…places to go to ground, and places to get food or supplies that are open all night long while you're on the run."

"We've been considering that in trying to work up a profile on him," Price said. "There's not much. Baldero has no criminal record. No known associates in the drug trade or with fringe political groups. No legal records of any kind, apart from a custody battle working its way through the courts. He's got an estranged wife and a three-year-old daughter, living in Texas."

"So," Bolan said, slamming the big car's accelerator to the floor and rocketing around a slow-moving panel truck as he gained on the gunfire ahead of him, "we've got a former CIA cryptographer who's got himself into something so bad that it's worth putting holes in half the state to kill him. The question is, what?"

"That's what has the Man worried, Striker," Price said. "More than the need to put a stop to these attacks, and the unrest they're generating, we need to know what's behind it. It could be much worse. It's almost *certainly* much worse."

"Got it, Barb. I'm closing now. We've caught a break, it seems. Have Bear and his team stand by to analyze any intelligence I might—"

The cargo van that cut across Bolan's path was traveling nearly eighty miles an hour.

Bolan could see the van's grille bearing down on him as it barreled straight for the driver's door of his sedan.

The headlights shone very bright.

Bolan had a fraction of a second in which to react. He did the only thing he could do—he whipped the steering wheel hard to the left.

The dirty white cargo van blew past him on his passenger side, sheering off the car's side mirror in a small maelstrom of plastic shards and silvery slivers. The rear end of the big car broke free, losing traction through the violent maneuver. The back of the vehicle came around, and Bolan found himself skidding through a complete 180-degree turn. The smell of burning rubber filled the car as he fought the steering wheel and the brakes, riding out the skid and narrowly missing a passenger car as he crossed the double line and barreled through oncoming traffic. The Crown Victoria finally jerked to a stop on the shoulder of the opposite side of the road, facing back the way Bolan had come.

He wasted no time. Snatching up the canvas war bag that contained his gear from Kissinger, he threw it over his shoulder and was out of the car in a heartbeat. As he moved, he drew the Beretta 93-R pistol from its custom leather shoulder holster. Flipping the selector switch to 3-round-burst mode, he rounded on the van, which had come to a screeching halt half on the sidewalk a dozen yards from his own vehicle.

The side door of the van slammed open. A man shouted furiously at him, his features twisted in rage. In his hands was the futuristic-looking assault rifle. The muzzle of the weapon spit flame.

Bolan hit the pavement painfully, his right hand at full extension before him. The 3-round burst of 9 mm bullets caught the shooter under his chin and folded him back on himself, where he disappeared in the dimly lighted interior of the cargo van. Bolan had time to roll sideways before several streams of what his ear identified as rifle fire converged on the pavement where he'd just been, spraying him with sharp pieces of asphalt.

The soldier recognized his attackers' language readily enough. He had spent more than a little time operating covertly in cities like Tehran. It was Farsi, also known as Persian, the most commonly spoken of several languages in Iran and Afghanistan.

Very curious, he had time to think, with the incongruous detachment that often occurred in his mind when his body was engaged in the well-remembered and deeply ingrained mechanics of battle. The Executioner was nothing if not a thinking soldier, and his mind was always active, always analyzing the fluid and unpredictable rhythm of lethal combat.

Rising to a half-crouch, Bolan took a two-hand grip on the 93-R and glided heel-to-toe around the rear corner of the van, using the vehicle as cover. Predictably, shots began punching through the windows of the rear doors, but the angle was awkward and the gunners inside couldn't get a clear shot.

He heard footsteps and saw feet wearing desert-sand-colored combat boots hit the pavement on the side of the van, as the men within piled out. They were shouting instructions to one another in Farsi. Bolan's command of the language wasn't up to interpreting it, certainly not in the rapid, clipped tones they were using, but it didn't matter; the intent was clear. They were trying to coordinate their efforts to kill him.

Whoever these shooters were, there was no way they weren't related to whatever had been happening across Virginia—though how a witness could have confused men of Persian descent with Asians, he could not say and would not bother to speculate. The Executioner was painfully aware that whatever vehicle or vehicles these men had been chasing and shooting at, as well as however many more vehicles full of gunners there might be on the road between Bolan and the presumably fleeing Baldero, were now well beyond the range at which he could reacquire and pursue them. There was nothing he could do; he had to deal with the immediate threat, or he wouldn't be alive to continue with the mission.

It had only been by the blind luck of the battlefield that he had stumbled across the rolling gun battle in which he was now involved. Whoever these shooters were working for, whatever the connection to Baldero, erasing them and removing them from the combat equation was the one possible option.

Bolan threw himself flat again, lined up on the row of feet on the other side of the van and held the 93-R sideways to aim below and across the big vehicle's undercarriage. Then he triggered several 3-round bursts.

Two of the men dropped, screaming, their ankles shattered. Bolan put a burst into each one of them, ending their misery. Then he was up again, coming around the front of the van.

The driver was still in position, holding a pistol that looked like a SIG-Sauer. Bolan put a single round through the glass and reloaded on the move, swapping the 20-round magazine for a fresh one from his shoulder harness.

There wasn't much time. The police would be on the scene before long, responding to what would have to be countless phone calls about the war going on in the middle of the street in this mixed commercial district. His Justice credentials would put him above suspicion, at least eventually, and Brognola could always intervene on his behalf if he got embroiled with the locals, but it would cost time, and time was what he didn't have. He could hear the combat clock ticking in his head.

He heard the second vehicle moving in from behind him; the throaty roar of the heavy cargo van was unmistakable. There were still shooters from the closer van to deal with, so he focused on those, maneuvering to put this threat between him and the newer group.

Risking a glance around the corner of the near van, he sighted down the driver's side flank. Two men using the engine block for cover returned fire from where they crouched by the van's grille. Bolan ducked back just in time, as bullets sparked and ricocheted from the metal of the rear corner of the vehicle.

He considered going for foot shots again, but he dared not place himself prone as the other group moved in from the passenger side. Bolan was already outnumbered and was going to be outflanked, if he was not careful.

The soldier reached into the war bag and found the familiar cylinder of a smoke grenade. The metal was cool to the touch. He drew the canister, popped the ring and let the smoke bomb fly into the midst of the enemy gunners.

The cloud of acrid purple smoke that erupted was a tribute to Kissinger's skill with ordnance of that type. It immediately enveloped the shooters, obscuring their view of Bolan. They began firing blindly through the smoke. The Executioner hurried, moving to circle their position. As he did so, he drew the Desert Eagle from its hip holster and jacked the hammer back.

The first of the shooters burst from the cloud of smoke, assault rifle blazing. Bolan put him down with a single shot to the head from the big .44 Magnum pistol. The next man came, and the next, but they were blinded by the smoke, shooting wildly, their rounds far off the mark. The Executioner stood his ground and, gun in each hand, shot each man as he cleared the cloud of purple haze.

The gunners weren't stupid or suicidal. As soon as they figured out what was happening, the parade of half-blinded men stopped.

Then a grenade rolled out of the smoke.

Bolan didn't pause, didn't deliberate and didn't question his instincts. He simply kicked the bomb under the closer van and ran.

The explosion rocked the cargo van, pushing the nose up into the air as if the vehicle were rearing back on its hind axle. Thrown onto his stomach on the asphalt, Bolan felt the sudden wave of heat on his back. The breath was forced from his lungs and he lost his grip on his weapons. The spray of glass, plastic and metal fragments pelted his neck with tiny needles. There was no time to check himself for injuries, though he felt blood trickling down the back of his shirt.

Some sixth sense, some combat instinct—or perhaps just his awareness of the nature of battle—warned the Executioner that death was coming for him. He rolled over onto his back in time to see another man stagger through the last wisps of purple smoke. He had no weapon that Bolan could see. Blood trailed from his ears and his face was burned. He had been too close to the explosion, apparently.

Fixing Bolan with a hateful glare, the wounded man came straight for him. Bolan crabbed backward but had no time to regain his feet. The olive-skinned man landed on him, causing pain to shoot through Bolan's battered ribs and up his lacerated back.

Fingers wrapped around Bolan's throat. The weight pressing down on his stomach forced from him what little breath he had managed to regain. Suddenly he was fighting simply to draw air, dark clouds swirling around the edges of his vision.

The man on top of the soldier was screaming in what might have been Farsi. It might also have been simple gibberish; he was clearly mad with pain. Bolan could see burned skin peeling from his attacker's face as the man roared his fury.

The Executioner's hand fell to the right front pocket of his blacksuit pants. There, clipped inside his pocket, was a tactical folding knife with a wickedly serrated hawkbill blade. Bolan's hand clenched around the textured plastic handle of the knife and yanked it free. As he did so, his thumb found the hole cut into the blade. He snapped the folding knife open and heard it lock into place.

The attacker's eyes widened as the blade flashed into his view. Then he screamed. The Executioner brought the serrated blade down and across the man's arm, working his way around the arm closer to his strong side. As the grip on his neck loosened, Bolan arched his back, ignoring the pain it caused. He threw the shrieking would-be killer off his chest and rolled over with the man, taking the dominant position.

The attacker was struggling to pull a pistol, apparently forgotten until that moment, from his belt. The Executioner's knife flashed once across the man's neck. He died, loudly, and Bolan released the knife, snatching the gun from its position in the dead man's belt.

Bolan rose to a half-kneeling position, checking his immediate field of vision and also risking a quick glance behind him. His trained, experienced gaze missed nothing—a quick look was all he needed to assess the situation. Then he ejected the magazine in the pistol, checked it and slammed it home again. Press-checking the pistol showed him a 9 mm round in the chamber.

The pistol, which Bolan had first thought to be a SIG, was in reality a PC-9. He needed no reference book to call up what he knew of the handgun. Battlefield experience had made him a walking encyclopedia of firearms data. The weapon was an unlicensed, unauthorized copy of the SIG-Sauer P-226—and it was manufactured in Iran.

His own guns were somewhere on the pavement, but there was no time to look for them. Figures were moving through the pall of black smoke cast by the twisted, burning wreckage of the first van. Bolan detected police sirens in the distance. The clock had run out. He was out of time, his targets slipping that much farther out of his reach, and *this* fight wasn't over.

Again employing his gliding, half-crouching fighting gait, the Executioner moved through the smoke to the opposite side of the remaining van. A man holding an assault rifle saw him and drew down on him. Bolan put a single 9 mm round between his eyes.

As he closed on the van and on the shooter's position, Bolan caught movement from the corner of his eye. He turned in time to intercept a rush of men rounding the passenger side of the van's grille. He fired quickly in a two-handed grip, first one, then another, and another. The first man fell with a bullet through his brain. The second was clawing at his throat where Bolan's 9 mm bullet had pierced his neck; the light was already fading from his eyes as he fell to his knees, gurgling and trying to scream. The third man took a slug directly through his heart. He was dead before he finished falling over.

There were still shooters beyond the van, the last of the armed resistance. They fired at Bolan, but the angle was wrong. Both the soldier and his enemies were using the van as the only available cover between them, which meant the gunners had to be content with chewing away from the flanks. Asphalt and paint chips filled the air, ripping past with a noise like tearing cloth, while empty brass littered the street and curb. Those were not the sounds that worried Bolan most.

The police sirens were growing louder; the local authorities would be on the scene in moments. The Executioner did not dare let that happen. Deadly experience, always his guide, told him that the first thing the Farsi-speaking shooters would do, if confronted by police cars, would be to turn their automatic weapons on the law-enforcement officers. Though perhaps well-trained and well-equipped, the cops would not be prepared to roll straight into a barrage of automatic gunfire. Even a S.W.A.T. team would have a hard time coping with so sudden a burst of violence, and the new arrivals were likely road patrol responding to numerous calls of shots fired.

The Executioner had cut a bloody swath through the ranks of the criminal underworld and the international terrorism scene during his endless war for justice. Regardless of the side of the law on which he operated—and he'd spent plenty of time exacting a righteous toll on society's predators on the "wrong" side of law and government, whenever that had been necessary to get the job done—he had done so while always respecting one rule above all else. He would not take innocent life, and he would not take the life of a law-enforcement officer who was simply doing his or her duty.

Given that, Bolan would no sooner allow those law-enforcement officers to stumble blindly into a killing field that was partly of his own making. It would be like herding cattle through the gates of an abattoir.

Bolan scooped up a fallen assault rifle and snatched two magazines from the belt of the dead man who had wielded the weapon.

The weapon was one he knew, but which he had not encountered often. It was a Khaybar KH 2002, a bullpup weapon based internally on the M-16 A-1 that looked like an ungainly cross between a Steyr AUG and a French FAMAS. He checked the rounds in the magazines by simple eye—this rifle fired the same 5.56 mm round as did the rifles that had inspired its design.

The Executioner took only a second to verify that the weapon was chambered and ready. Then, holding the rifle close to his body, he threw himself prone and rolled across the pavement, his head pointing toward the enemy.

The enemy gunners saw him but had been waiting for a target at waist level. Their fire went high and, before they could compensate, Bolan unleashed a series of tightly controlled bursts from the muzzle of the futuristic-looking rifle.

The 5.56 mm rounds tore through the knot of men, splaying them in every direction. One of them screamed; the others died silently. The screamer managed to clench the pistol grip of a small submachine gun as he left this world. The rounds it discharged caused Bolan to flinch from a fresh spray of sharp asphalt shards that drew blood from his cheek.

The gunfire echoed away at last. Bolan got to his feet, the Khaybar stock tight against his shoulder. He moved quickly and cautiously forward and around the vehicle, checking every direction with fast glances side-to-side and behind him. There was no more movement from among the gunmen. He had killed them all.

The first of the police cars reached him, LED light bars strobing, sirens howling. Immediately, officers threw open their doors and leveled their pistols at Bolan, shouting for him to drop his weapon and make no sudden moves.

The Executioner held the rifle up over his head in both hands. The shouting continued.

"I am an agent of the United States Justice Department," he said very deliberately, emphasizing each syllable so they could hear him over their sirens. "I have engaged these men to—"

"Shut up!" one of the officers ordered. Two more came up on either side, all of them keeping a prudent distance from the soldier. "Place your weapon very slowly on the pavement!"

Bolan did so. "I am an agent of the United States Justice Department," he repeated patiently. This was nothing he had not endured before. "I have credentials and identification on my person."

"Hands behind your head!" the officer shouted again. "Interlace your fingers! Do it now!"

Bolan did as instructed. He was seized, cuffed none too gently and then patted down. The frisk was halted abruptly when the officer realized just how many pouches and pockets the blacksuit had, and how many of these had something lethal in them. His war bag, still slung over his shoulder, was brimming with things that would give an ATF agent apoplexy. Bolan could only imagine how the police would react when they got to that.

"Holy shit," one of the cops muttered. "This guy is loaded." He called for the other two officers, the ones who had braced Bolan. The soldier was half pulled, half dragged upright and escorted to a police cruiser. There, his war bag was placed heavily on the trunk as the officer resumed the frisk. The two backup men held their weapons on Bolan the entire time.

The sat phone Bolan carried, which was now on the trunk in a growing pile of his personal weapons and accessories, began to vibrate, skittering across the trunk a few inches as it did so.

That was probably the Farm. Once he spoke to them, word would get passed to Hal Brognola that he would need to intercede, yet again, on Bolan's behalf. The big Fed had logged far too many hours of his life calming anxious representatives of local law enforcement who did not take kindly to Bolan's wars waged through their bailiwicks.

Brognola was probably in the middle of having breakfast. Bolan imagined this would ruin his appetite.

Bolan sat in the open side doorway of the one intact cargo van, turning the small submachine gun over in one hand. He had his sat phone open and against his ear. Barbara Price's voice, as sexy as ever to him despite her all-business tone, came clearly across the scrambled link to Stony Man Farm.

"Cowboy verified it based on the photos you snapped and transmitted to us," Price said. "The weapon is an MPT9K—an Iranian copy of the Heckler & Koch MP-5 K. That makes it a clean sweep, Striker. He says your identifications of the rifle and the pistol you picked up were dead-on."

The Executioner was not surprised. After a tense half hour during which he had been allowed, on the strength of his Justice credentials, to contact Brognola, who then placed an immediate call back to the police department and local FBI offices, Bolan had been released. The grudging attitude of the officer who had cuffed him hadn't prevented the man from doing his job in an efficient manner, especially after his own superiors had contacted him and doubly confirmed what Bolan had tried to tell him.

The soldier's weapons and personal effects had been returned to him, at which point Bolan asserted Justice's jurisdiction, at least at the outset. The officers had stood back while he used the digital camera in his sat phone to snap pictures of the dead men, their equipment, and the scene of the destruction Bolan had wrought on the street. He had transmitted them to the Farm for analysis.

A crime-scene team had since taken over, scouring the area and tagging and bagging anything that wasn't nailed down. Once he had his photographs, Bolan had no further need to take charge of the aftermath of the fight. He was content to let the Farm run diplomatic interference behind the scenes. A great deal of covering up of the true nature of the shooters would likely have to be done, if reports of further terrorist shootings were to be averted. Already, several media crews were being kept at bay by uniformed officers wielding collapsible roadblocks and what appeared to be several miles of yellow caution tape.

"I'm done here," Bolan informed Price.

"We'll transmit directions to your phone's GPS application, as usual," Price said. "I assume you're headed toward Norfolk."

"Yes, since that's the direction our boy was heading when I stumbled into this. You can get the field team moving there, if you haven't already."

"They're well on their way," Price confirmed. "They'll beat you there and will act as our advance eyes and ears. Maybe we can yet get you ahead of the Iranians."

"Iranians?" Bolan asked. "We have confirmation?" While all the weapons the shooters had used were Iranian, and rare enough in the United States, he would not assume the gunmen had been from Iran without some sort of verification. It was one of the oldest "plausible deniability" tricks in the book to equip a team with weapons not traceable to the nation fielding that team, or traceable to a completely different nation, in order to misdirect the enemy and confuse the issue should members of the team be captured or killed.

"That's affirmative, Striker," Price said. "We have identities back on half a dozen of your dead men, the ones who have Interpol records. All are Iranian black bag operators. Three were officially dead long before they ever met you. We've made some discreet inquiries through the usual channels, but of course the Iranians wouldn't give us the time of day or a straight answer about this even if we were on *good* terms with them. It's pretty obvious that you're facing an Iranian-sponsored hit team, though what they could want with Baldero is still a mystery."

"Something's bothering me, Barb," Bolan said.

"What is it?"

"It's no small thing to sneak a small army of commandos into the country. Logic dictates that if you did, you'd equip them locally. Weapons are readily enough come by here, after all, and even illegally obtained automatic weapons would be more easily purchased through stateside contacts than smuggled into the U.S., wouldn't they?"

"It would depend, Striker," Price said. "If the Iranians were in a big hurry, they'd equip their team domestically and send them in as quickly as possible, the consequences be damned. It's not as if we enjoy a good relationship with them."

"True," Bolan said. "But if that's the case, how did they get in? This many men, carrying weapons and explosives? There's a huge hole in our border somewhere, Barb."

"That's not really news, Striker," Price said, "but I take your meaning. I'll see if Bear and his people can come up with something. We'll start prodding other agencies, especially DHS, Coast Guard and Border Patrol to see if we can come up with something."

"All right," Bolan said. "I've lost enough time already. Time to get moving."

"Good hunting, Striker."

"Out," Bolan said. He closed the phone.

The officer who had first cuffed Bolan, named Sheddon,

had been watching the Executioner from out of earshot, giving him time to finish his phone call. When the soldier closed the phone, the cop walked up to him and tried to smile. The result was genuine, if a bit sheepish. Officer Sheddon held up a plastic evidence bag in which Bolan's bloody folding knife was sealed.

"Agent Cooper?" Sheddon asked, gesturing with the bag. The Justice Department identification that Bolan had flashed liberally to the officers on scene said that his name was "Matt Cooper." He had worn many aliases in his fight against society's predators. The exploits of Agent Matt Cooper would be somewhat legendary by themselves, if somebody had the time and the security clearance to start tallying them up.

"Yes, Officer?" Bolan said.

"They've cleared me to return your weapons to you, sir," Sheddon said. He pointed to one of the cruisers. "See Officer Ames, the one with the blond hair, there. He's got them locked in his trunk, sir. You sure you don't want medical attention?"

"Thank you, no." Bolan said. "I assume you have no more questions for me?"

"None that they'll let me ask, sir," Sheddon said. He looked irritated and a bit rueful, but he was a good cop and didn't appear to be holding any serious grudges. "I'm afraid they want the knife, though, sir. Evidence."

Bolan raised an eyebrow. "Then why not the guns?"

"Plenty of shell casings and bullets to be had." Sheddon shrugged. "You know how it goes. They don't want this—" he gestured with the evidence bag again "—walking off if it was used in one of the, er…deaths."

"I understand. You're doing your job."

"Yes, sir."

"Keep at it." Bolan nodded to him, stood and offered his hand. Sheddon shook it; his grip was firm.

"Sir?"

"Yes, Officer?" Bolan asked, looking back over his shoulder.

"Good luck with…whatever it is you're doing."

"Thank you, Officer."

It took Bolan only a few minutes to gather up his gear, check the Crown Victoria for damage and get on the road toward Newport News. Once in motion, he pressed the gas pedal as close to the floor as he dared, weaving through traffic with skill and determination. He was already far behind the curve, but there was no point in delaying further. Until he knew otherwise, his quarry was more likely than anywhere else to be in Newport News, Hampton, Norfolk, or beyond it. That meant he needed to be there, too, and soon.

He set the cruise control and, though he knew it was dangerous, spared a glance at his phone. He scrolled through the data the Farm was transmitting to him, calling up each image as it downloaded. There were brief personal biographies of the men for whom identities had been dredged up, and complete dossiers on two men not pictured. Bolan read in fits and starts as he switched his attention from the small screen to the road and back again. These were the Farm's best guess at the likely leaders of such an Iranian strike group. It was a guess based on past Iranian intelligence ops and what Stony Man's almost prescient computer team could tell him of known Iranian terror operatives—those operating with the nominal sanction of their frequently rogue state's government.

The two dossiers were for men named Hassan Ayman, likely the senior member of an Iranian field team assigned to stir up trouble in the United States, and a Marzieh Shirazi, whose name Bolan remembered from several different terror bulletins in Europe. Each man had a file as long as Bolan's arm. Shirazi was linked to several bombings of targets in Israel, where he had a close working relationship with the PLO and, more recently, with the Palestinian government that incorporated many high-ranking PLO figures, each man among them a murderous terrorist in his own right. Shirazi was small and squat, with a prominent brow, and dark, beady eyes pressed into a face that looked like it had stopped a brick at some point in Shirazi's teenage years.

Ayman concerned Bolan more. He had no definitive terror incidents or murders assigned to him but, according to the file, he had long been rumored to be an extremely high-ranking official in Iranian intelligence. He was implicated in scores of deaths of civilians and nominally military targets alike, both in Israel and during the Iran-Iraq war. This last started in 1987. Apparently Ayman was believed, by the Farm's team and as independently theorized by CIA analysts, to have been instrumental in several high-profile atrocities during the tail-end of Iran's "imposed war" with Iraq. If either Ayman or Shirazi was on scene, or if both of them were active in the here and present, on the streets of the urban United States, things would only get more bloody.

The big question remained: what did Iranian black-ops assassins want with a single former CIA cryptographer, a young man who had never, according to his file, worked as a field agent or on anything resembling a project related to Iran? This much was included in the data the Farm had sent on Baldero. It was a puzzle, and Bolan did not like puzzles. They pointed to incomplete information, and incomplete information, though a common problem in the field, was the most frequent cause of lost engagements. To gain and keep the initiative in combat required that *he* surprise his enemies. He did not intend to be on the other end of the exchange.

He was burning up the road, having passed Hampton and Newport News without incident, debating whether to cycle back and forth between them and Norfolk when his phone began to vibrate. The Farm would know he had reached the next city, of course; they were tracking him through the SAASM-compatible GPS tracking module in his phone. The Selective Availability Anti-Spoofing Module technology was the U.S. Military's answer to GPS positioning. It ensured that, while his phone could be tracked by the team at Stony Man Farm, giving Price and her people up-to-date location data as Bolan traveled the country, no enemy could do the same, nor could false position data be transmitted to the Farm to misinform Kurtzman's cyber team.

"Striker," he answered.

"Striker, we have a mission-critical update," Price said without preamble. "We are transmitting new coordinates to you as we speak. The advance field team has been combing likely spots for Baldero to go to ground, including local motels and gas stations. They have a pickup truck parked behind a Dumpster at a motel on the North Military Highway. They say it's full of bullet holes."

"Registration?"

"The truck was reported stolen in Charlottesville yesterday," Price said, "and now it's wearing a set of stolen license plates swapped from a similar Chevy S-10, also in Charlottesville."

"Coincidence?"

"There's that word again," Price echoed.

"I'm on it," Bolan said. "Out."

It took him another fifteen minutes to reach the address, guided by the GPS directions in his phone. When he was close to the location, he stowed the phone and slowed, doing his best to stay inconspicuous. He found the motel and reconnoitered as quietly as he could, cruising around and hoping his interceptor and its missing side mirror wouldn't scream "law enforcement presence" to Baldero if the man were watching and had reason to fear legal interference. Bolan was not a police officer, of course—he was a soldier. Baldero would not know that, though. To the fugitive Baldero, Bolan would represent the law, and any man running from so many shooters would either welcome rescue or fear capture. The situation would be very tense until the Executioner knew which way Baldero would break.

There was no sign of the advance field team. They would have pulled out to some discreet distance once word got out that a Stony Man operative was on the way. The team's job was not combat and its mission was to remain undetected, to go unnoticed as long as possible. Getting drawn into a firefight was not its purpose; the unnamed, faceless analysts who had sent so much after-action intelligence Bolan's way thus far could only continue to do so if they stayed out of the way. That was fine with the Executioner. He preferred to work alone, whenever possible, and if there was a firefight to be had, he was content to bring it to the enemy.

He found the truck right where he had been told to expect it, hidden in the lee of a pair of industrial-sized trash containers behind the motel. He parked behind it, blocking it in, nose-out in case he needed to put the Crown Victoria into action quickly.

The truck's engine was still ticking. It had not been parked for long and was still shedding excess heat from what had to have been a breakneck drive. Bolan could smell burning brakes and hot rubber, the unmistakable odors of a vehicle that had been pushed to its limits.

He had his canvas war bag slung over his shoulder. Before he moved on the motel, he paused to open the bag's large cover flap. Inside was the mini-Uzi he had first noted when making a cursory inspection of the care package from Kissinger. He withdrew the weapon, loaded one of the 30-round box magazines from the bag and placed the weapon on the hood of his vehicle.

He recounted the other explosives and lethal surprises in the bag, as well as taking stock of the loaded magazines for the Uzi. Kissinger had thoughtfully provided several 20-round box magazines for the Beretta 93-R, its 9 mm ammo compatible with the Uzi. There were a handful of loaded mags for the .44

Magnum Desert Eagle, too, and a few boxes of ammunition for both weapons.

Finally, he withdrew a small item he had at first overlooked. It was a rosewood-handled boot dagger in a leather sheath with a metal spring clip. He withdrew it, examined the four-inch, double-edged blade and resheathed the knife with a mental nod. Then he clipped the sheath inside his waistband in the appendix position, where he could draw it with either hand readily enough. His windbreaker covered it, barely, as it concealed his other hardware in their holsters.

As he went to pick up the mini-Uzi from the hood, a slip of paper fluttered from his sleeve, where it had been caught following his reach into the bag. Bolan scooped it up quickly, checking to make sure he was still unobserved from his vantage behind the garbage containers. Then he unfolded the paper.

Wear them in good health, it read in handwritten print. *Stay alive.* It was signed, simply, "Cowboy."

Bolan shoved the slip of paper deep into his pocket. He picked up the Uzi and, holding the weapon low against his leg, moved in on the motel. Once he was in the shadow of the building itself, he took out his phone and texted a message to the Farm's quick-contact number, which would display on a readout in the Computer Room, asking for room number intel.

Almost immediately, the responding text message came back, probably typed by Price herself: "Bear says man matching Baldero's description checked in room 112. Grnd floor, East."

That would mean the Farm, or someone on the advance team reporting to the Farm, had checked with the front desk. Whether overtly using government authority, or covertly using some ruse, the Farm had determined that a man who looked like Baldero had checked into room 112, which Price was informing him was located on the ground floor of the east wing of the double-winged building.

He made his way there, watching the doors and room numbers tick past in descending order as he went by. He was doing his best to ignore the gun held against his thigh. It was an old trick of role camouflage; if the gun wasn't anything *he* noticed, a bystander might not notice it either. While there were always exceptions, Bolan knew from experience that most people simply didn't look at the individuals around them. The majority of people walked through life in what one late, famous self-defense expert had called "condition white," a state of blissful unawareness of their surroundings. Bolan was counting on that. It wouldn't do for some particularly aware citizen to notice his weapon and call the police, perhaps tipping off Baldero that he had been located.

He found room 112 and pressed himself against the wall next to the door. Reaching out with one hand, he rapped on the door quietly, using the back of his left fist.

"Yeah?" came a voice from inside.

"Housekeeping," Bolan said. "You want fresh towels?"

There was no reply from inside. Bolan could hear the occupant, presumably Baldero, shuffling around within. If it wasn't his man, no harm would be done. If it was, however, he needed to take control of the situation right now. If he could get Baldero to open the door without causing a scene, he could quietly remove the man from the premises and take him into custody. Getting Baldero under wraps was the first step in stopping the shootings that were causing so much trouble, and in unraveling the mystery regarding *why* the shootings were happening.

"Sir?" Bolan asked again. "If you'll just open the door—"

Just then a shotgun slug tore a hole the size of a quarter through the heavy motel door.

Straddling an upholstered wooden chair with his arms resting on the chair's back, Yoon Jin-Sang focused the binoculars for a better view of the large, dark-haired man who had just entered the shelter of the motel's second-floor overhang, sticking to the shadows. The man moved with unmistakable, deadly grace, like a panther. Yoon suppressed a shudder. He thought perhaps it was as they had feared, and the dreaded night-killer rumored in the reports trickling slowly down from military intelligence were true. If they were, he could believe that this man, the man he had just glimpsed in the binoculars' view, was the night-killer. He did not say so. He knew the feelings of Kim Dae-Jung on the subject and did not wish to agitate his "superior." When he spoke, he was careful to keep his tone subdued.

"He is here."

"The large American?" Kim's voice was too casual, almost indolent. The large, muscular man leaned back in his chair and paused to stare at the ceiling, as if he did not care.

"Yes, the same man," Yoon said. "He is approaching Baldero's room."

Kim did not reply. Yoon banished the sigh before it could

escape his mouth. His *true* superiors in military intelligence had given him his orders in no uncertain terms. He was to do his best to see to it that Kim carried out the mission with which he was tasked. Given Kim's dangerously unstable nature, that might prove difficult, but it was not, they emphasized, considered impossible. Kim had been selected from the ranks of intelligence's disgraced operatives because he was expendable and because he still had family members who ranked highly in North Korea's military command and intelligence structure.

It would suit the family honor of all concerned if Kim's wild nature was harnessed where he could do the most damage among the hated West, and that was deemed to be the United States. If Kim died spectacularly, sacrificing himself in that self-destructive manner that so characterized him, this was deemed so much the better. Even their leader was at least dimly aware of Kim's volatile nature. Certainly the man had disgraced himself and potentially his family publicly enough in North Korea, his eccentricities finally culminating in atrocities against North Korean civilians that even the government and its military enforcers could not ignore.

For the mission to be an unqualified success, Yoon had the unenviable task of keeping Kim restrained in order for them to capture this American, Daniel Baldero, and spirit him out of the country. Kim had to live only long enough for the team to acquire Baldero; if he died thereafter, that was best. Yoon had been informed by his superiors, in fact, that Kim was *not* to survive the mission. If that meant he were to meet with an accident on his return to Pyongyang, well, that was what it meant. The problem was not seeing to such an accident—the problem was keeping Kim under control long enough for them to get that far. He was dangerous, unstable and unpredictable—but Kim was also a deadly warrior, a berserker with no fear. They would need him before the mission was over, especially if this night-killer was truly involved. Yoon swallowed again, his throat very dry.

The three of them—Yoon, Kim and the woman, Hu Chun Hei—sat in the upper-story room of the motel across the street from the one in which Baldero had only just rented a room of his own. It had not been difficult to secure the space, even in a hurry. It had been more difficult to conceal their field teams in their trucks in the hotel parking lot, for Yoon feared they were entirely too obvious sitting there in the American sport-utility vehicles. They had already risked flushing the prey once, and they could not afford to be discovered, not yet. For the plan to succeed, they had to remain unseen until one of the foreign teams had acquired Baldero. Then Yoon, Kim and their men, along with Hu, would swoop in and steal the prize, like an eagle taking a fish in its claws. The Americans would look like fools, Kim would die a hero, and Yoon would return to a promotion and much political currency in Pyongyang.

Already, their surveillance had shown them much, and their contact within the Americans' government had told them even more. It was, Yoon thought, truly astounding, the lengths to which the traitor American had gone to keep them apprised of the situation this man had helped create. He cared only for money, it seemed, and Pyongyang had transferred vast sums to him to secure his cooperation. More had been promised. Whether the man lived to spend it would be up to Kim, more than likely, and Yoon cared only that the man live to the limit of his usefulness. After that, Kim could indulge his baser instincts to his heart's content. No one would have to know—what was one more fat, dead American? Yoon laughed at the thought and wondered if Baldero understood the extent to which his fellow American was willing to sell him to the enemy. Probably Baldero did not. It was not important.

The American government man had, in fact, fed Yoon's people a steady stream of intelligence since helping to bring them and their equipment, undetected, into the country. It was easy enough for the fool, as he was telling them primarily of their competition—other teams, similar to their own, from nations hostile to their interests and to the United States, whom the American had similarly helped to enter the nation. The North Koreans had paid him the most, and promised yet more, and thus the North Koreans enjoyed the privilege of the traitor's further betrayal of the rest of his customers. How such a man thought himself anything but an animal, loyal to no one and nothing, Yoon could not fathom. Surely the man knew he had no honor, and that his actions earned him no esteem among those he greedily served against the land of his own birth? It amazed and disgusted Yoon, who nonetheless was determined to use the traitor until he could be used no more. Distasteful as this business was, their team could not have succeeded without this assistance from within the ranks of the American government.

Most important was the tracking device. Kim, looking sullen and bored, sat on the room's other chair toying with the small plastic-shelled unit, which showed on a GPS overlay that their quarry was in the building they monitored from across the street. Yoon had no doubt that the American had provided the other foreign kill-or-capture teams with similar devices, for it explained easily how the Iranians and the French had repeatedly found Baldero, as Yoon and Kim themselves had originally found the man. Fortunately for all of them, those Iranian and French fools had yet to do anything but shoot up large portions of the state. Baldero had proved to be a wily prey and had evaded them every time, once set to running. They would keep finding him, most assuredly, but with any luck the Israelis would intervene and either evade the others or neutralize them for good. Once that happened, Yoon would suggest that Kim and his team move in, and they would steal Baldero for themselves.

To face their competitors directly would be suicide, and suicide of a type in which even Kim was reluctant to engage.

They had many men, and they had weapons, but they were outnumbered by the other teams. No, they had to wait for the odds to change in their favor, the fortunate benefit of such a delay being that the other nations, were they discovered, would likely take any blame to be spread. Yoon and whoever did survive the mission could return to North Korea's shores with no blood on their hands and no possibly irritating diplomatic problems following them—problems that Yoon was certain the West could use as convenient excuses to foist more onerous sanctions on an already unfairly beleaguered North Korea.

Failure to obtain Baldero simply was not an option. No less than the leader himself had expressed a desire to possess the man, and thus it fell to Yoon to make sure this occurred. Were he to fail in that, his only other option would be to make sure Baldero died, and that might yet lead to a long, slow death by torture once he returned empty-handed. Much was riding on this. If Baldero did not end up in their possession by the time it was finished, Yoon just might kill Kim and then himself. He would take his own life to spare himself pain; he would take Kim's both from a sense of duty and for sheer spite.

On the face of it, it was daring, almost insane. A single American citizen held the key to potential military superiority for each nation to whom the program of his creation had been brokered. To Yoon's knowledge—and he believed it to be reasonably complete—those nations, those *customers*, were Iran, dissident or covert elements within the French government, similarly rogue operatives formerly of Israel's Mossad, and of course North Korea.

The Iranians were fanatics and fools; they posed no real threat. There were, however, a great many of them. At least, there had *been* a great many of them. Trailing Baldero using the tracking device to stay undetected at a safe distance, they had almost stumbled directly into the battle that had erupted in Williamsburg. It was there that Yoon had caught his first look at the night-killer of the legends. The more he thought about those apocryphal reports, the more he thought this man, this implacable killer who had scythed through the Iranians as if they were so much fragile wheat, was the man of which North Korea's security agents had so long whispered. It was said that more than once such a man—tall, with dark hair and blue eyes, a killer so formidable that his passing was like that of a lightning storm—had fought the interests of the leader's military and intelligence operatives, defeating them every time.

Even to breathe the nickname, "night-killer," was to risk summary torture by the most zealous of the leader's internal security forces. But if such a man, rumored to be an American mercenary or commando, truly existed, would he not appear when blood and gunfire erupted with the force of an invading army so very close to the seat of the American's government? It seemed likely to Yoon. They had watched the night-killer destroy the Iranian force the man had encountered, then they had resumed their pursuit of Baldero, tracked him to his motel and taken up their observation posts once more. It was only a matter of time before the French or the Iranians, or both, arrived to try to kill him once more, and then the chase would begin anew.

That had been the plan, but Yoon was no longer sure. If the night-killer took Baldero, he had much less confidence that his team could take the prize from this deadly foe. He was, suddenly, glad of Kim's presence, for if any man were monster enough to face the night-killer of legend and kill the man, it would be Kim. He was just crazy enough, and just dangerous enough, to match this unwelcome enemy.

The shotgun blast, when it came, deep and unmistakable, almost caused Yoon to jump. He was glad he did not; he did not wish to appear weak before his two companions. Kim looked up from the tracking device, interest and something like arousal crossing his face. Sitting on the edge of the bed, the woman, Hu Chun Hei, tossed her long black hair to the side in a reflexive motion and stopped manipulating the folding knife she carried.

They waited for long minutes, holding their breath. Nothing happened, and no one emerged from the hotel. The tracking unit, which Yoon could read from across the room, showed that Baldero was still inside the motel across the street. There was nothing to do but wait. Yoon tried to concentrate on the binoculars once more, hoping to catch a glimpse of Baldero or the big American who may well have met his end before the muzzle of the unseen shotgun.

Kim made a sound of disgust and slumped sullenly back into his chair, staring at the wall. It was at these times that he was most dangerous; when he grew still, it was never long before he exploded into violent movement, without warning and without provocation. In a way, Yoon could not blame him. The following, the waiting without action, were taking a perceptible toll on all of them. Only Hu remained impassive, but then, she was always inscrutable.

The sound of the knife whirling in the woman's slim fingers told Yoon, who did not look back at her, that she had gone back to toying with the blade. She had been playing with the sharp, talon-shaped folding kerambit knife she carried since they had entered the room, silently spinning the vicious little weapon in endless circles from the finger ring in the handle. Back and forth, back and forth, completely around, then back and forth again—the knife's movements were almost as hypnotic, were he to look at it, as was Hu's beauty. She ranked highly in military intelligence, he knew, though no one in Kim's unit was quite certain how high. She was Kim's woman. That much had been made clear to him. As a result, none asked, and none dared question him…or her. Whatever arrangement Hu herself had with Kim and with their superiors was her business. It would, ultimately, be her neck, too.

Yoon had no instructions concerning Hu. She worried him, for if her loyalty was to her lover, Kim, and not to military intelligence and the leader's government, she might interfere when it came time for Kim to die a hero's death. If that happened, he would have to kill her, too, and he did not like the idea of incurring political debts to unknown individuals farther up the chain of power than he. Unfortunately, he had no choice in the matter. His primary and secondary mission objectives remained as they were regardless.

"I am going to call that fool, Tontro," Kim announced abruptly. He removed a prepaid wireless phone, untraceable and readily available in the United States, from the pocket of the American jeans he wore. His black T-shirt, the jeans, and the American jungle boots he wore were a kind of uniform, among the North Korean team members. They were cheap, not very conspicuous and functional in the warm climate of Virginia. Yoon and Hu were similarly attired, though Hu's clothing was significantly tighter.

"Tatro," Yoon corrected automatically. It had become a mantra, and now Yoon suspected Kim did it on purpose, simply to nettle him. Little things like that were the man's idea of humor, Yoon supposed, though he found the madman distasteful even at the best of times, and perfectly offensive when he was trying to be funny.

"Tatro." Kim nodded, smiling his sickly, lopsided smile. He put his phone to his ear after redialing the number with a single press of his thumb. Yoon heard him and the American government man, the traitor James Tatro, exchanging meaningless pleasantries.

Yoon wondered if Tatro had the slightest idea just with whom he was in bed. North Korea was considered, laughably, a "rogue nation" among the Americans, though of course they *would* propagate such misinformation in their efforts to bully the leader's people into submission. But the Americans, on the whole, especially those in their government, were curiously squeamish about violence. They would drop bombs on smaller countries from thousands of feet in the air, but the idea of actual blood flowing through their own fingers revolted them. Such was the stuff of Kim's most pleasant dreams. If only this Tatro knew with whom he dealt, he would understand that he had truly signed a deal with someone he should consider a devil.

Kim's family disgrace had started with a few easily covered-up murders. They had been servants, for the most part, and the occasional party or factory worker. Some had been transients. A few had been prostitutes, despite the leader's best efforts to eradicate such practices from the streets of his nation's fair cities. Kim had a sickness, one that drove him to need to kill as regularly as some men ate a heavy meal. The longer he went without indulging his impulses, the worse the expression of those dark inner desires was when it finally came to fruition. Forced by his family to give up his depredations, Kim had lived in what for him most surely had been agony, spending several months locked away in his family's state-designated dwelling in Pyongyang.

When he finally escaped, he killed the person sent to guard him, an older cousin from his own family. Then he had escaped and murdered several families living in the public housing a few blocks away. It had been very, very difficult to cover up the evidence of those murders, to expunge all trace of those family's many relatives and their connections to North Korean society in Pyongyang. Many threats had been made. Many citizens had been sworn to silence. Still many more had simply disappeared. It was not long after that, Yoon knew, that Kim had been consigned to this mission, a disgrace both to his family and to his work within military intelligence. He was an expendable, vicious animal who, once he served his purpose, would be put down like the rabid dog he was.

Yoon looked forward to that much of the mission.

"You have not informed us of something," Kim finally said into the phone. Yoon could hear the other end of the line almost as clearly as Kim. The dangerous Korean had the volume of his phone set as high as it would go, the result of hearing loss in his good ear caused by a firearms "accident" when he was a teenager.

"I don't understand," the government man replied. Tatro's reedy voice grated on Yoon's already frayed nerves.

"You have not told us of all we face in our mission," Kim said flatly, his tone hinting at deadly reprisals.

"But I have," Tatro insisted. "I gave you full information on the size of the Iranian team and on the equipment I helped them smuggle in. The French team was delayed this morning when one of their trucks broke down, my spotters tell me, but they're well on their way to you if they're not there already. The Jews are around somewhere. That's all."

"There is another. A lone American. Big. Dark hair. Well armed. Very dangerous. The idiot Iranians spotted him on their trail and tried to kill him. Who is he?"

"I don't have any information about a single operator," Tatro whined.

"You have been paid a very, very large sum of money, American," Kim threatened. "You were promised much more when we secured this fool whom you have so readily sold us. Do you think you can betray us now? With a single phone call, I can ruin you. I can see to it that your countrymen lock you away for the rest of your miserable life…or I can find you myself and see to it that you suffer for the very short span of whatever brief life I allow you to have."

"I don't know who it—"

"Find out," Kim said. "Before it makes a difference to me. Or do not ever let me find you."

Tatro was trying to say something when Kim hung up on him. Yoon shook his head very slightly. He would be glad when this was over.

Bolan stood very still as the shotgun blast echoed from within Baldero's room. His right hand stood poised to draw the Desert Eagle from its IWB holster; the .44 Magnum rounds would punch through the door easily. He did not, however, want to risk killing Baldero. There was too much still unknown, about the shootings and about Baldero's role in fleeing them. Taking him alive would go a long way toward solving some of this bizarre mystery that surrounded the "terrorist attacks" across Virginia.

"Daniel Baldero!" he said. "I am an agent of the United States government. Put down your weapon and open the door, slowly."

The sound of a pump-action shotgun being racked was very loud from the other side of the door. "Fuck you!" someone shouted. "You're trying to kill me!"

"Baldero, I am *not* trying to kill you," Bolan said. He decided to gamble a little with a judicious application of the truth. "But," he said, "it is very, very important that you allow me to take you into custody so that we can prevent your death at the hands of those who *are* trying to kill you."

"So let's see some ID, as if that matters!" the man inside shouted.

"I could show you my identification," Bolan said, "but would it mean anything to you? If I was an assassin using that ruse, I'd show you a fake ID and then put you down. What you don't seem to realize is that I could have shot you through this door at any moment in the last sixty seconds. Now open the door, Baldero. Quickly. We probably don't have a lot of time now that you've got the neighbors' attention."

There was a pause. The door opened to the length of its security chain, a bar in a brass slider. The unshaved face of Daniel Baldero, framed by long, black hair, stared out from the gap. The gaping muzzle of the shotgun was visible below his face.

"Put it away," Bolan ordered. "I'd rather not get my head blown off just coming in the door."

Baldero, looking irritated but also concerned, pushed the safety lever on top of the pistol-grip Mossberg's receiver. He lowered the shotgun and glared. "Just who are you?" Then, looking at Bolan and back at the shotgun, he leaned it against the wall by the door. Bolan waited as Baldero closed the door, removed the slider and opened it again. The soldier ducked in and closed the damaged door behind him as quietly as he could, for all the difference that was likely to make.

"My name," Bolan said, "is Matt Cooper. I'm with the United States Justice Department."

"Care to tell me just why your buddies have been trying to off me?" Baldero demanded. He balled his fists at his sides. In person, he was a big man, almost a match for Bolan's height and thicker through the chest, with muscles in his meaty forearms that betrayed the tension in his stance. His hair reached to his shoulders and gave him an almost feral appearance. He had dark, angry eyes and the bearing of a brawler, not a deskbound computer jockey. Well, Bolan knew that computer techs came in all shapes and sizes. The fact that this one might have broken a jaw or two wasn't an earth-shattering shock. In fact, if Baldero was a survivor, it accounted for how he'd managed to stay ahead of the Iranians all this time.

"Exactly what is it you think is happening?" Bolan asked. "And talk while you pack. We're leaving."

"Leaving for where?"

"Anywhere else," Bolan stated. "If I could find you, someone else can, too." The soldier would call Stony Man and arrange for a safehouse. Then it would be a simple matter to move Baldero there until the appropriate authorities could pick him up. They wouldn't know just whom those authorities should be until they'd unraveled the strange story behind the shootings, but that would keep. At the moment, Bolan was painfully aware that they were exposed here, sitting ducks for anyone who might have heard Baldero's shotgun or who happened to spot the bullet-riddled pickup truck.

"Someone else, who?" Baldero asked.

"I want to know who you think that is," Bolan insisted.

"Isn't it obvious?" Baldero said. He grabbed a duffel bag from the floor and began shoving into it the few clothes that were already strewed on the threadbare motel carpet. "The government is trying to kill me because of the program. They've got what they want, and they've decided they don't need me. So I get screwed, and then I get dead."

"Wait," Bolan said, putting up a hand. "Back up. Program? What program?"

"The program," Baldero said, as if that explained everything. "The damned *program,* man. The encryption program I created. The one I tried to sell. You know? The reason the government wants me dead?"

Bolan just looked at him for half a second. "You wrote an encryption program?"

"Yes!" Baldero said, throwing up one hand in frustration. "The frigging fuzzy logic encoding algorithm used to—" He paused abruptly. "You have no idea what I'm talking about, do you?"

"No," Bolan said.

"Oh, that's just great." Baldero shook his head. "That's just freaking beautiful."

"Come on," Bolan said. He grabbed the man by the shoulder and gave him a shove toward the door. "We're leaving."

"All right, all right," Baldero groused. "Enough with the shoving already. Jesus. You wearing jackboots, too?"

"Combat boots," Bolan said flatly. "Shut up and go."

Baldero went to grab for the shotgun, but Bolan beat him to it, snatching the weapon and carrying it in his left hand as they left the motel room. They made it around to where the truck was parked. If anyone noticed them, no alarm was raised and no shots were fired.

Bolan didn't like it. He had the very uneasy feeling he was being watched. He couldn't quite put his finger on why—it was just an instinct, a tickle between his shoulder blades. It had saved his life more than once.

Baldero moved to the truck, but Bolan urged him on. "We'll take my car," he said, jerking his chin toward the Crown Victoria.

"That's a cop's car," Baldero said. He eyed Bolan suspiciously.

"Get in," Bolan said. Baldero did so, muttering.

It's going to be a long drive, Bolan thought. He put the shotgun on the floor behind the front seats and then climbed behind the wheel, slamming the door behind him. The engine roared to life when he turned the key. Startled by the throaty roar of the engine, Baldero looked at Bolan sharply, something like appreciation in his expression.

Bolan pulled out of the hidden drive and pushed down the accelerator, moving quickly through the relatively light side-street traffic until he got back onto the nearest highway. He reached for his phone and was about to hit the speed dial for the Farm when he noticed Baldero checking a small smartphone of his own. He tapped briskly away with his thumbs on the PDA's tinny QWERTY keyboard.

"What is that?" Bolan asked as he drove, looking from the road, to Baldero, to the road again.

"My phone," Baldero said with a sneer. "You *have* seen a phone before, right?"

Bolan ignored the gibe. "Has it occurred to you that you're being pursued by a team of foreign military operatives who are trying to murder you?"

"Yeah," Baldero said, not looking up from the smartphone. "I thought it was my own government's military operatives, but same difference. I was using the university lab to do some compiling. They know me there, and their machines have more juice than my home system. Next thing I know, there's bullets everywhere. The same bunch has been on my ass ever since."

"And did it not strike you as odd that they keep finding you? Finding you, that is, and shooting up everything around you, putting the entire state on terrorist alert?"

"Not really," Baldero said. "I'm one guy, alone. They must be spotting me and relaying over to their guys, somehow. I thought they must have lo-jacked my car somehow, but I tried stealing another and it didn't make a difference."

"That would be the pickup?"

"Yeah."

"Grand theft auto wasn't listed in your dossier."

"No, but it was a great game." Baldero grinned. When Bolan did not react, other than to shoot him a stone-faced glare, the younger man shrugged. "I was CIA, man. You pick up stuff from the field agents sometimes. I lost the key to my ride once, and one of the agents showed me how to wire it up. I thought it might come in handy some day."

"Why did you quit the CIA?" Bolan asked. He whipped around a slow-moving minivan and accelerated, concentrating on the traffic. He had no real destination in mind; he just wanted to put distance between them and Baldero's stolen truck.

"A month ago," Baldero said, "I wrote something. Well, finished writing something. It's something I've been working on, you know, on the side. Probably the most innovative encryption program ever created, I don't mind telling you. I figured, I could give it to the Agency and to the government, sure...but what would I get out of it? Maybe a medal. Maybe a note for my file. Hell, maybe even a promotion. And then right back to my desk for another sixty- to eighty-hour work week, at least until the next time the terror alert turns a different shade. Why bother? I figured I'd sell the program and make a fortune. Live out the rest of my life in peace. So I started to get my ducks in a row, and then I put in my notice. I'm not contract. The Agency hired me for my skills. I figured I'd go use them in the private sector."

"What's so special about the program?"

"It can't be broken," Baldero said confidently. "Not unless I write the decryption program."

"And that is?"

"Up here." Baldero tapped his head. "Without what's up here, and in here—" he gestured with the smartphone "—where I keep a memory card with my notes, well, there's no way the program's ever going to be cracked. It can't be. I've got to do it."

"How is that possible?"

"Do you know anything about programming languages?" Baldero said. "Encryption methods? Logical heuristics?"

"Not really."

"Then take my word for it," Baldero said. "But you got to figure, a program that can do that, it would be worth a fortune, right? It would make PGP look like Morse code, man. Like nothing."

"Have you had that phone with you the entire time?" Bolan asked.

"Of course, I have," Baldero said. "And I know what you're thinking. But if they're tracking me, it's not through this phone. This is an advanced model. Encryption on encryption, and not traceable like your average wireless. It's a generation ahead of the smartphone the President of the U.S.A. carries, man. It's more advanced than that satellite phone you're toting around, too."

Bolan looked down at the phone still in his hand.

"Yeah," Baldero said, "I know what that is. I've been around, man. Encryption and communications security is my business…what did you say your name was?"

"Matt Cooper," Bolan said. "So there's no way they could be tracking you through that?"

"No way at all," Baldero said. "Completely impossible. First thing I checked, too. Took it all apart and gave it the once-over. There's nothing there that doesn't belong there, and no way they could be tracing my signal through the network."

"Well, they're tracking you somehow," Bolan said.

"Yeah. Who did you say they were? I figured the government was going to off me to get the program before I could cut a deal."

"At this moment," Bolan said, "you appear to be the target of an Iranian death squad."

"Iran? No effing way."

Bolan said nothing. He maneuvered through and around another slower moving knot of traffic. "Why did you think the government was after you?"

"Who else?" Baldero shrugged again. "I never figured on freaking Iran, man. Beats me how they'd be involved in this."

"Could they have bought your program? You said you tried to sell it. If they kill you before you create a decryption program, they've got a method of sending coding transmissions that nobody can intercept. That would be a valuable thing to any government, and to any terrorist organization."

"No way, man. No. Not on your life. I'm no freaking traitor, Cooper. I made sure there was no way my program would get into the hands of somebody hostile to the United States."

"How would you do that?"

"Well, I made some…anonymous inquiries online. Then I… Cooper. Cooper!"

Baldero was pointing. The highway had widened to two lanes, and in the left lane, next to them, a Dodge Nitro had pulled up even with Bolan's position. The passenger-side window was rolling down.

Bolan had been aware of the vehicle pacing them. He had been expecting another attack from the moment they had left the motel. There was too little chance that the enemy were blindly stumbling on Baldero every time; they had to be following him and reacquiring him somehow. If it wasn't his phone, then it was a bug somewhere on his person. The problem was, they could practically strip-search him and still not find a device of that type. That meant there was no choice but to fight their way clear until they got some breathing room.

The man inside the pacing vehicle brought up a Colt submachine gun and pointed it straight at them. Bolan hit the brakes. The burst of 9 mm fire burned the air above the hood of the Crown Victoria.

Traffic was too heavy for an extended battle. If he tried to engage the shooters here, he would risk innocent lives. That was not acceptable. The soldier scanned the highway ahead of him, found an opening and punched through, grinding the gas pedal to the floor.

The sedan's engine growled. Bolan cut behind another passenger car rather than in front of it, to lessen the chance that the gunmen would fire through a civilian vehicle to get to Baldero. Then he powered through the exit.

The exit ramp was very long, but steeply curved. At its center was a grassy "median" of sorts that was more like an island of forest, with a stand of trees. At the extreme arcs of its curves, it had guardrails to prevent traffic from leaving the road, but there were large gaps before and after them. Bolan kept his speed at the absolute maximum the curve would bear, the Crown Victoria just at the verge of breaking loose and sliding across the asphalt.

The driver in the Dodge misjudged both the speed of the vehicle and the angle of the curve. Bolan watched the rearview mirror as the wheelman in the pursuing truck lost control. Baldero was yelling something, but Bolan did not listen; instead, he pressed the accelerator all the way down again.

The Queen Victoria pushed up and over the curve of the ramp, thundering through the field beyond. Bolan gripped the wheel tightly, fighting as the car spun its wheels on the high grass and the soft earth beneath it. Baldero was thrown from his seat so violently that he bumped his head on the roof of the vehicle. He cursed, long and loudly.

The Dodge rolled through a path roughly parallel to the sedan. The windshield spiderwebbed. The engine screamed as the wheels spun through empty air. The Nitro came to rest on its roof, rocking slightly, at a forty-five-degree angle resting on the slope of the grass hillock abutting the outer curve of the ramp.

Bolan brought his car around with difficulty, fighting for traction on the grass. He reached the protection of the stand of trees.

"Take the shotgun!" Bolan ordered. "Go into those trees and stay there. If anybody comes at you who isn't me, shoot them."

Baldero, to his credit, didn't argue or talk. He just threw open the rear passenger door, grabbed the Mossberg and ducked into the trees with it. There weren't many and it wasn't much in the way of cover, but it would have to do.

Bolan drew the mini-Uzi from his bag and cocked it. He was looking right at the undercarriage of the Nitro. Taking a two-handed grip on the Uzi, he watched as men started to crawl from the vehicle. The nearest still held the Colt SMG with its skinny 9 mm stick magazine poking out from the middle of the AR-15-profile well. The man shouted something and brought up the weapon.

Bolan stitched him with a short, well-placed burst from the Uzi. He held the trigger down once more and sprayed a trail of Parabellum rounds across the undercarriage to the gas tank. Never one to fire indiscriminately, he laid down a withering fusillade now for effect. Something sparked. Flames rose up. He emptied the Uzi completely.

The gas tank finally erupted in a ball of flame. It engulfed the nearest man, who staggered to his feet and then ran madly, screaming and wildly triggering his submachine gun as he was burned alive. Bolan quickly changed magazines in the mini-Uzi, dropping the spent stick in his bag, and grimly put a single mercy round in the head of the human torch.

There were two more men still moving, and one who had fallen still by the hulk of the burning Dodge. Bolan shot down the first one and then backed toward his vehicle. The second man tried to pursue. It was obvious he was walking blind; blood from a gash on his head was in his eyes. He fired randomly from the Colt SMG he carried, a duplicate of the one wielded by the first gunner. Bolan couldn't afford to wait to see if he managed to fire into the not-so-distant passing traffic, so he punched a single bullet through the man's forehead.

"Cooper!" Baldero screamed from the trees. "Help!"

Bolan turned and ran. He threw himself past the Crown Victoria and then the trees, knowing he was risking catching a slug himself, heedless of the danger. If what Baldero had told him was true, the man's life had to be preserved. If he died, the secret of his encryption code might die with him, leaving a dangerous security risk in the hands of a rogue nation. There was no telling the kind of damage a terrorist-sponsoring nation like Iran could do if it had in its possession an unbreakable means of coding transmissions among its operatives, across a network of terrorist cells.

Should Iran or whoever else might have the code sell it to an organization like al Qaeda, the damage would be multiplied a thousand-fold. International terror groups across the globe would be emboldened. Counterterror intelligence operations monitoring terrorist "chatter" and gathering intel from those terrorists' communications would be hamstrung, to say nothing of the damage done if the code were possessed by an enemy nation capable of fielding its own conventional army, such as Communist China.

Bolan spotted Baldero standing in the middle of the small

stand of trees. The soldier froze. Very slowly, he lowered the barrel of his Uzi.

There were five men standing there, all of them dressed in black in what Bolan considered Army-Navy surplus modern—sweaters, cargo pants and hiking boots. Beyond them, at the other end of the group of trees, Bolan saw a second dark-colored Dodge SUV, this one a Durango. The men standing before him held AR-15s or M-16s—it was impossible to tell for certain at that distance—and one of them had another 9 mm SMG variant of the Colt weapon. There had been two groups, obviously; one had hung back, circled around and come from behind. It had simply been their good luck that they had run into Baldero. At least they hadn't killed him immediately. Bolan noticed the pistol-grip Mossberg shotgun on the ground a few feet from the man.

One of the men spoke quickly. Another answered. Bolan caught just enough of it to identify the language.

They were speaking French.

One of the two men who stood at either side of Baldero pointed the muzzle of his assault rifle up under Baldero's chin. "Weapons down," he said, his accent thick. "Do it or we kill him."

"You're going to kill him anyway," Bolan said. "That's why you're here, isn't it?"

The slight widening of the man's eyes gave away something, but Bolan wasn't sure what. Baldero looked like he wanted to say something, but the flash-hider pressed under his jaw kept him quiet.

Bolan did not loosen his grip on the mini-Uzi, but he kept it pointed toward the ground. He took a half step closer to Baldero, judging the distance to the gunmen. These men were of much lighter complexion than the Iranians he had faced. Was it possible they *were* French, or French-speaking mercenaries?

"That is far enough!" The gunner who had been doing

the talking started to bring his weapon on line with Bolan's head.

The soldier threw the mini-Uzi at him.

It was an act of insanity and desperation, throwing a loaded submachine gun like that. Bolan trusted the grip safety and the soft earth beneath their feet to prevent the weapon from chopping him or Baldero off at the shins when it hit. The talkative gunner with the French accent ducked instinctively, and the eyes of the other men momentarily followed the Uzi as it arced through the air.

That was all the distraction the Executioner needed.

He fired a vicious, low side kick that snapped the knee of the man to Baldero's left, who screamed and toppled. Then Bolan threw a palm heel up under the chin of the talkative shooter. He heard the man's jaw snap shut and then a nasty crack as something in the man's neck popped. He crumpled.

Baldero threw himself on the ground, grabbing for the shotgun. The Executioner jerked the 93-R pistol from his shoulder holster while drawing the .44 Magnum Desert Eagle from its Kydex holster in his waistband. The Beretta disgorged a 3-round burst while the big Magnum-caliber hand cannon belched flame.

One of the shooters folded in on himself, the 3-round burst blowing his chest to shreds. Directly across from him, Bolan's .44 Magnum round had punched a tunnel through the head of one of his partners.

The man with the broken knee started to drag a pistol from under the canvas jacket he wore. Bolan shot him with the Desert Eagle and he pitched face-forward onto the grass.

The fifth man dropped his weapon and made a mad dash for the Durango. Baldero was up with the Mossberg, but Bolan waved him off. "No," he said. "I want to try to take him alive."

Baldero swore vehemently; Bolan ignored him. He glanced

around to make sure his charge was in no danger—there were no shooters still on their feet, and Baldero had the shotgun if he needed it—then pursued, shoving his guns back into their holsters as he did so.

It was possible the man he'd palm-heeled was still alive, but it was also possible he was dead. Bolan wanted very much to have a live prisoner to interrogate. These men weren't the Iranians, unless they were French contractors to the Iranian hitters. The Executioner needed to understand their involvement. So far, nothing about this mission made sense, but what little Baldero had already told him was starting to form as a concrete idea in the soldier's mind.

Bolan caught the fleeing man as his prey reached the Durango's driver's door. The Executioner grabbed two handfuls of the commando-style black pullover the man wore and yanked him back.

The back kick that shot out at Bolan nearly took him square in the groin. He sensed it coming at the last moment and turned, taking the blow on his thigh, almost causing his leg to buckle.

The man twisted and hit the ground, then leaped up, bending backward at the waist to surge to his feet without using his hands. Bolan backed up half a pace. This one, it seemed, was belatedly a fighter.

Bolan brought up his hands in a loose fighting stance. His opponent swore at him in French and began throwing high, fast kicks that whistled past and even over his head. Bolan recognized the style—it was savate, a French martial art characterized by its dynamic foot strikes.

Bolan let the man continue to throw kick after kick, wearing himself out. He ducked and slipped as necessary. The soldier took one and then another glancing blow across the shoulder and the side of his head, which did him no favors but weren't particularly painful. His opponent was getting tired.

As they circled each other, Bolan could again see Baldero's position in the small clump of trees, and he noticed that the Virginia State Police were starting to arrive, which didn't surprise him. He hoped the interference Brognola had run for him that morning would continue to hold for this latest encounter.

The kick that slammed past the Executioner's head and clipped his ear would have taken his head off had he not been just a bit faster than the savate man. Bolan had not truly let his attention wander—he never did that in battle—but he *had* underestimated the man, who had not been as winded as he first appeared. It was time to end the exchange and stop playing around.

Bolan waited, watching and dodging or blocking with his own legs as the savate fighter fell into a pattern of forward and side kicks. Then he waited for just the front kick he wanted—and caught it, dropping an elbow into the leg as he fell to his own knee. His weight, combined with the elbow blow, inflicted crippling pain just above the man's knee joint. Bolan's opponent howled in pain and fell to the ground, clutching at his injured leg.

The man rolled over. Bolan, realizing what was happening, once more grabbed him by the shoulders and yanked him back onto his back.

It was too late.

The man's teeth were clenched. He began to convulse. Bolan caught a whiff of bitter almonds.

Cyanide.

Disgusted, Bolan left the man where he'd fallen. Potassium cyanide–induced cardiac arrest would kill him; it might be killing him even then. There was little the Executioner could do for him in any case. He hurried back to where he had left Baldero. With the state police on the scene, it might be possible to get EMTs to the fallen man in time to treat him before the cyanide stopped his heart.

He located the officer in charge on-scene and identified himself, giving his Justice credentials a workout. The cops didn't seem terribly comfortable with Bolan's heavily-armed presence, but they let him be. They told him an ambulance was arriving in response to multiple motorists' reports of a rollover accident. When the paramedics got there, the officers pointed them to Bolan's poisoned foe at the soldier's urging. Once he'd seen to that, he once again started taking digital pictures of his fallen enemies. He paused to check the one he'd struck with the heel of his palm, but there was no pulse. He retrieved and checked the mini-Uzi after he'd done so.

"I think that guy's dead, man," Baldero said, pointing from where he sat. He was leaning forward in the front passenger seat of the Crown Victoria, with the door open and his feet on the ground. "That was pretty hard-core, man."

Bolan had no response for that. He examined some of the discarded weapons and snapped some more photos before transmitting the images to the Farm.

"You, like, taking trophy shots, or what?"

"Or what," Bolan said flatly.

"You're a real conversationalist, Cooper," Baldero groused.

"Why aren't you dead?" Bolan shot back.

"They grabbed me and told me to shout for help." Baldero shrugged. "I figured I was better off with you nearby than with you not nearby, so I did it."

"Probably wanted to take me alive, just like I wanted one of them," Bolan said.

"What, to, like, torture you and make you talk?"

"Probably."

"Hard-core," Baldero said again.

Bolan said nothing. He came around and got back into the car, started the engine and hit the gas. Baldero barely had time to pull his feet in and slam the door. With some difficulty, the soldier got their vehicle back onto the road, though they were nearly bogged down in something that wasn't quite mud before the rear wheels finally grabbed asphalt again.

Bolan speed dialed the Farm.

"Price, here," the mission controller said. "Striker, we're processing the images you sent. Are these—"

"Another party heard from," Bolan said. "They were speaking French and carried American-made weapons."

"We're on it, Striker. Our field team says you acquired Baldero?"

"Yes," Bolan said. "He's here with me."

"We'll route you to a safehouse."

"You may want to reconsider," Bolan said. "Baldero says they're chasing him because he's written and sold a code. Something very special, an almost unbreakable encryption method."

"I didn't say *almost*," Baldero said.

Bolan ignored him, but then he did glance over as he drove. "How did you say you sold this thing?"

"I was trying to tell you," Baldero said. "I did some checking. The Net is anonymous, or it's anonymous up to a point. I made contact with someone who said he could find a buyer. We traded emails for a while, and I checked him out, traced his IP address, all the usual stuff. He works for the Department of Homeland Security, or he's attached to them somehow."

"And?" Bolan asked.

"And nothing. That's all I know."

"You sold a revolutionary encryption code to an anonymous person on the internet?"

"Well, yeah," Baldero shrugged. "He put ten grand down and promised a lot more, transferred the funds right to me. I figured if anybody could make sure the code was only sold to people we could trust, you know, friendly countries, it would be somebody at DHS, right? I mean, doesn't that make sense?"

Bolan glared at him. "Barb, did you catch all that?"

"Yes," Price said. "I'll have Bear check it out."

"We're being tracked somehow," Bolan said. "Baldero swears it's not his phone and, based on what little I know of it, he might be right. I'm not sure how they've bugged us, but we're running hot until we get enough room to do a thorough search. Baldero says the reason he's wanted dead is to prevent him from writing the decryption code, to keep his program valuable to those who already have it. If it's fallen into the hands of the Iranians, that makes sense. They kill him, they've got an unbreakable cipher they can use to coordinate acts of terror."

"Which means Baldero must live to create the decryption code."

"Yes, if he's as good as he says he is, and if his program does what he says it can do."

Baldero glared; Bolan continued to ignore him.

"Hold on, Striker. Let me check with Hal."

Bolan waited. Price came back on the line moments later. The next voice Bolan heard was that of Hal Brognola.

"Striker," the big Fed said. "Barb says you have him."

"I do," Bolan said. He gave Brognola a summary of what he and Price had discussed so far.

There was a pause. "Jesus, Striker," Brognola said. "It's worse than we thought."

"I'd say it is." Bolan nodded, though only a curious Baldero could see him.

Bolan heard Brognola tapping some keys on his own computer terminal. Price could also be heard in the background, giving hushed instructions to the Stony Man team. Finally, Brognola said, "Striker. Listen very carefully. There's a computer analysis facility maintained by the Justice Department. It's here in D.C. I want you to bring Baldero there. Barb will send you the relevant details."

"All right," Bolan said.

"It's clear," Brognola said, "that whoever Baldero thinks he sold the code to, it's out now. We don't know how far it goes. If the Iranians have it, anybody could, from a handful of tinpot dictators anywhere up to global terror networks. We cannot allow them the luxury of secure communications. It undercuts one of our most powerful weapons in the war against terror. Baldero has to write the decryption code. He *has* to live to do it."

The data receive icon was already flashing on Bolan's phone; the information was being transmitted through the secure satellite link from the Farm. "I'll get him there, Hal," Bolan vowed.

"Striker, what about a chopper? Barb could have you extracted," Brognola said. "We could have you flown directly to D.C."

"Negative," Bolan said. "We're up against a small army of hitters packing military hardware. If they've got even one rocket or surface-to-air missile among them, or they just get lucky, Baldero and I will be sitting ducks in a chopper while they're tracking us. On the ground, if they come at us, I can at least fight them."

"He's right, Hal," Price said.

"All right," Brognola said. "It's up to you, then, Striker."

"We'll see you in D.C. Striker out."

Bolan swore under his breath.

"What now?" Baldero said.

The soldier had, as he drove, been monitoring the rearview mirror. They had picked up yet another persistent tail, and this one was making no attempt to hide its pursuit. The late-model silver Jeep Grand Cherokee flashed its brights at Bolan, coming up along the passenger side.

"Oh hell," Baldero said. He made as if to duck in his seat. Bolan saw he had put the pump-action shotgun back on the floor behind him, and now he was reaching for it.

"Hold on," Bolan said. "This is something…strange."

The woman driving the Jeep rolled down her window. She

was beautiful, with long, straight dark hair, fine features and large, dark eyes. She motioned toward a sign on the highway ahead of them:

Rest Stop—12 Miles

"I think she wants us to pull over," Baldero said.

"Yeah." Bolan nodded.

"We going to?"

"Yeah," Bolan said. "When the shooting starts, hit the floor and stay there."

"Shooting? Why the hell are we pulling over if there's going to be shooting?"

"We need information," Bolan said, "and if I'm right, she's got some."

"That's not all she's got," Baldero said.

Bolan ignored him.

The rest stop was large and, thankfully, not very busy when Bolan pulled the sedan into a parking slot at the far end of the lot. He immediately got out of the car, motioning for Baldero to do the same. As was often the case at stops like these, there was a picnic area on the grass opposite the lot. Several wooden picnic tables sat nearby in a sheltered pavilion. Bolan motioned his charge forward. He was very aware of the silver Jeep pulling into the lot and parking a few spots away from his borrowed Crown Victoria.

"Sit down on the far side," Bolan told Baldero. "Roll under the table if it gets hairy."

"This is just wood, man," Baldero complained, rapping the picnic table.

"Better than nothing," Bolan said. "Now shut up."

Baldero glared but did as he was told.

The woman who approached him was even more stunning up close than she had been at seventy-five miles an hour. She was slim but curved in all the right places, with a wary, deceptively casual gait that hinted at extensive martial arts or combatives training. She carried a Glock pistol in her hand, held low by her leg.

Bolan immediately went for his Beretta 93-R. She made no attempt to bring up her gun.

"The Uzi would be better, I think," she said. Her lilting, lightly accented voice was low and sultry. She wore a form-fitting coverall of some kind, the tight pant legs tucked into low-topped boots. The four men who fell into step behind her, emerging after her from the Jeep, wore a mixture of casual clothes doubtless intended to make them inconspicuous. That made sense; there was no way the woman with them would ever be anything but noticed.

"And just what does the Mossad want with me?" Bolan challenged.

Her neatly plucked eyebrows went up at that. "You are very good with accents, Mr.…?"

"Cooper," Bolan said. "Justice Department."

"You are very good with accents, Mr. Cooper, to be able to determine organizational loyalty from them."

"No," Bolan said. "I'm just not stupid. You *are* Israelis, right?"

"You guessed that part right, yes."

"I thought so. Would you mind telling me what you're doing here?"

She laughed. It was a sexy, musical sound that Bolan wouldn't have minded hearing again. "I think, first things first, Mr. Cooper. We are here to help you."

"Oh?"

"Yes," she said. "You are about to be attacked again."

Bolan was on his feet, Beretta in a two-handed grip, scanning for threats.

"They are there." The woman pointed. In the distance, two more sport utility vehicles, a Chevy and a Ford, were cutting through traffic, making for the exit to the rest stop. "Our friends the French are not quite through with you. They have a great many people in the country, I am afraid. Almost as many as the Iranians."

Bolan looked at her. He wanted to ask her what she knew, how she knew it and how she had found them, but there was no time. The enemy was approaching and it was time, once again, for war.

"I am Ayalah Rosen, by the way," she said, tossing her lustrous dark hair back. She press-checked her Glock and then rapidly said something in Hebrew to the men behind her. Two of them ran for the rest stop building.

"Where are they going?" Bolan asked.

"They will herd any civilians away from the fighting," she said, "and remain to guard them should any of the French turn their guns on bystanders. I do not think it will come to that, but who can say?"

"Aren't the French, like, our allies or something?" Baldero said from under the picnic table.

"Shut up," Bolan and Rosen said to him in unison.

"Here they come," one of the two men who'd remained with Ayalah said.

The first truck jumped the curb. The two male Israelis exchanged a few more words in Hebrew and then produced Galil assault rifles from their Jeep.

All hell broke loose.

The Israelis opened up first, their Galils spraying jacketed bullets into the grille of the lead SUV. The second truck stopped behind it as the first one ground to a messy halt, smoke or steam pouring from under its freshly ventilated hood. Armed men, shouting orders to each other in French, began pouring from the vehicles. They carried more AR-15-type weapons.

Bolan was not about to stand toe-to-toe with so many shooters, not with Baldero protected by nothing but a picnic table. He made a judgment call and turned, leaving the beautiful Ayalah Rosen and her men to deal with the oncoming gunners. Crouching, he held out a hand to the younger man. Baldero took it and held on tightly as Bolan dragged him from under the picnic table and pushed him to his feet.

"Go, go, go," Bolan ordered. He shoved Baldero in the direction of the rest stop building. The cryptographer needed no further urging. He ran for it, with Bolan close behind.

The battle raged at their backs. A few slugs tore the pavement near their feet, but nothing got so close that Bolan had to worry Baldero would take one. Then they were at the doors to the rest stop building and through.

The two Israelis Rosen had detailed to herd the civilians clear were standing inside. They had Glock pistols in view, but no other weaponry. At the sight of Bolan with Baldero, they moved to block the way.

"Move it," Bolan said.

One of them said something in Hebrew. The other said in English, "I'm sorry, sir. We have orders. You may go, but he—" he jerked his chin at Baldero "—must remain behind."

"He's leaving. With me." Bolan's tone left no room for doubt.

"I do not think so," the Israeli said. He moved chest-to-chest with Bolan, looking him square in the eye. He was easily a match for Bolan's six-foot-three, two-hundred-plus frame, perhaps an inch taller and maybe thirty pounds heavier, all of it muscle. Clearly, he was a man accustomed to intimidating other men with his size. Bolan had seen the chest-to-chest posturing countless times before, always in those who counted on staring down their enemies rather than beating them down.

"Your people are fighting to help us," Bolan said, "so I'm going to be polite about this. Move out of my way and don't interfere. Mr. Baldero is an American citizen and I am an authorized agent of the United States Justice Department. Just who you are has yet to be determined. Don't interfere."

The bigger man stared him down, saying nothing.

Bolan whipped the back of his left hand, hanging loosely at his side, into the man's groin, driving the bone knob at his wrist into the man's crotch with a nasty snapping motion. As he did so, he ducked to the right, and the big Israeli's forehead impacted with Bolan's shoulder as the man bent forward in reaction to the pain. The Executioner slammed the butt of his Beretta 93-R across the back of the man's head at the juncture of his skull and his neck. He hit the floor with a bone-jarring crack that might have been his nose breaking.

Bolan extended the lethal-looking nose of the Beretta 93-R, his arm locked as he leveled the weapon at the face of the other Israeli. The little machine pistol was actually an older design, but it and others like it had served the Executioner well in the many battles of his endless war. At a press of his finger, a 3-round burst of 9 mm rounds would scorch the air before the weapon, destroying anything that happened to be in their path.

Some recognition of this fact flitted across the wide eyes of the second Israeli. He let his Glock dangle by the trigger guard.

"Don't do that," Bolan said irritably, reaching out to take the weapon, very carefully, with his left hand. "If it's chambered you'll put a round through the ceiling or yourself."

The Israeli swallowed. He said something Bolan couldn't understand. Then he tried again. "I have...not great English."

"Likely story," Bolan said. He put the Glock on the floor and shoved it with his foot. It skittered across the smooth, polished floor and came to rest at the entrance doors. "Get out of here, pick that up on the way and do what your team leader told you to do. Guard our backs, if you want to be helpful. But try to stop me, and I'll burn you down."

"I...understand."

Bolan watched the Israeli as he pushed Baldero through the back of the rest stop area, toward the bathrooms. They saw no civilians. There either had been none, or the two Israelis had succeeded in chasing them off.

"He's going to come right back after us," Baldero said.

"Probably," Bolan said. "But he'll see to his friend first, and it might occur to him that his comrades are fighting for their lives outside." They could still hear automatic gunfire coming in fits and starts from outside the building. "I'm betting he'll help them before he charges in after us alone."

"Did you kill that guy?"

"Not unless he's got a delicate constitution."

There was a burst of gunfire, this one much, much louder. It came from just outside the restroom area. "Get into one of the stalls, up on the toilet," Bolan ordered. "Stay out of sight as long as you can."

Baldero hurried to do as he had been told. Bolan, Beretta in hand, risked a look around the corner of the bathroom entrance.

Two of the supposedly French gunners had entered the building. The Israeli Bolan had left walking was lying dead on the floor, surrounded by a widening pool of his own blood. The shooters lowered the barrels of their guns to cover the other stunned Israeli who was on the floor.

Bolan couldn't allow them to shoot the man dead while he was unconscious. He didn't want to be responsible for a murder like that.

"Hey!" he shouted. "Over here!"

The gunmen looked up. Bolan pushed the Beretta out and squeezed off a burst that took the lead man in the neck. He fell back, his arms out, fingers splayed, gurgling in shock and horror. The Executioner tracked the second man and triggered his gun once more, blowing a neatly placed cluster of holes in the man's center of mass. The exit wounds left a bright smear of dark red blood on the tiled wall behind him as the corpse made an almost comically slow slide to the floor.

Bolan knelt over the Israeli he'd pistol-whipped. He slapped the man's face lightly. "Hey," he said. "Hey. Wake up. Snap out of it."

The Israeli's eyes fluttered open. Bolan put a finger to his lips. "Your gun is six inches from your right hand," he told the man. "Your partner was just killed by your French gunmen. If they're here, that means they've broken your leader's lines and they may well have us trapped in here."

The man's gaze hardened as he came out of his daze. "I will assist you," he said.

"I thought you might. Baldero does neither of us good dead. Am I right?"

"You are correct." The Israeli nodded solemnly. He looked at the three dead men on the floor.

"Abrahem did this?"

"No," Bolan said. "I did, after they shot him."

"I see." He looked at the dead men again, then to his partner once more. "You avenged him."

"I suppose."

"You stopped them from killing me?"

"Possibly."

"My name is Noam. I pay my debts."

"That's good to know." Bolan nodded, in a gesture that was almost a salute. He squatted quickly and picked up the dead Abrahem's pistol. "You need this?" He offered it butt-first to Noam.

"No." Noam shook his head. "I have mine. Take it."

Bolan turned on his heel and went to find Baldero. He called for the man as he entered the restroom.

"Here." Baldero opened the door to a stall near the end of the row.

"Come on." Bolan gestured to the translucent window at the far end of the L-shaped room. "We're going out the back."

"There's still a lot of shooting out there, man."

Indeed there was. Gunfire was raging from at least three corners of the building outside. Bolan judged that where they stood was the farthest from any of the pockets of shooting, which was as close to something like safe as they were going to get.

"Make a stirrup."

"What?" Baldero asked.

Bolan gestured with both hands and then pointed to the window. He took the suppressor for his 93-R from its pouch in his leather shoulder rig, screwed it to the end of the machine pistol's barrel and triggered a burst across the glass. It shattered and fell away. Bolan slapped the remaining shards out of the frame with the suppressor-equipped pistol, using it like a fireplace poker.

Baldero, swearing to himself, bent and made his hands into a loop. Bolan put his foot in the loop and, when the cryptographer heaved, used the boost to get up and through the window frame with his gun before him.

He landed heavily on the other side. The shooting was louder out here, but there were no gunners in sight. The rest stop building blocked his view of Rosen and the Frenchmen she and her team were fighting. Around the back of the building, several tractor trailers were parked in the extended portion of the curved parking lot that was designated for large commercial vehicles only.

When he was satisfied Baldero wouldn't be walking into a bullet, he reached up and gave the man his hand. The big, long-haired man grabbed Bolan's forearm in both his fists and scrambled up and out the window, grunting as he was half dragged, then half fell out the broken window. Bolan broke his fall as he reached the pavement, helping the young man get to his feet.

"I'm not built for climbing through freaking windows, man."

Bolan said nothing. He gestured for quiet and then pointed to one of the trucks. The weapons fire was starting to trail off, which either meant that the enemies were being beaten back, or that Rosen and her people had lost the battle. Bolan didn't intend to stick around long enough to find out which. Under other circumstances, he would have wanted to help Rosen, as he would have wanted to help anyone fight predators such as the gunmen who had done so much damage here. The Israeli woman knew the risks, however, and had volunteered for them. For that matter, Bolan was not certain she was not part of the problem. Certainly Noam had been very clear in his desire to stop Bolan from escaping with the cryptographer, which might mean the Israelis were hoping to capture Baldero for themselves.

Israel's interest in this, more generally, wasn't hard to figure out. Israeli intelligence was efficient and, of necessity, both thorough and ruthless. Surrounded by enemies and enjoying only intermittent support from their allies, the Israelis had become self-sufficient from the earliest decades of their nation's history. If the Iranians—and perhaps some faction within the French government—had come into possession of an unbreakable code, it wasn't unthinkable that Israeli intelligence agents would get wind of it, even before U.S. intelligence and Baldero's own former employer, the CIA, noticed what was happening. Given the threat posed to Israel by Iran on an ongoing basis, it was that much more likely that the Israelis would know of any Iranian attempt to achieve a military advantage, or to otherwise pose a threat to its neighbors' security.

"Now what?" Baldero said quietly.

"Stay here," Bolan told him. "Can you use a pistol?"

"I'm from freaking Virginia, man. Even the hippies carry pistols down here."

"Take this, then." Bolan handed him the Glock, again butt-first. "No safety." He press-checked it and made sure there was a round in the chamber. "It's ready to go. Point and shoot."

"I've seen a Glock before, Captain Obvious."

Bolan looked at him hard but let it go. "I'm going for the car," he said. "Stay crouched down here in the corner of the building, out of sight of the window." He paused. There were only a few pops and cracks of gunfire now. Whoever had won was cleaning up. "If the Israelis get here before I do, don't be afraid to be rude."

"How rude? Should I shoot 'em?"

"Try not to," Bolan said. "But look at it this way. How eager are you to end up in a foreign prison?"

"Not very."

"Then be rude," Bolan said, then left.

He could hear Baldero behind him, swearing.

Fortunately for all of them, the Israelis had beaten this new crop of shooters, French or otherwise. When Bolan came around the front of the rest stop, he was just in time to see Ayalah Rosen putting a round through the head of a fallen gunner. She stood over him, pointing her Glock, her left hand held to avert any spray, and performed the coup de grâce, looking for all the world like a bloodthirsty angel.

"Was that necessary?" he asked, climbing into his car. She looked up. "Wait, Cooper. We must talk."

Cars were speeding by the rest area, some of them visibly accelerating as they passed. Others honked their horns. It wasn't clear what the passing civilians thought. Some of them might have thought they were watching a movie being filmed, or a video game publicity stunt—something like that. There was no doubt in Bolan's mind that many of them had dialed 911. The state police would be along any moment. He was surprised they weren't already on the scene.

"Sorry," Bolan said. "No time." He put his foot on the accelerator and pulled away, circling the back of the rest area. Rosen called after him, but he couldn't hear what she said. It didn't matter.

Baldero eagerly jumped in when Bolan drove around the back of the building. The soldier only barely slowed the car. Baldero managed to scramble in while they were still moving, and Bolan floored the vehicle before the passenger door was closed.

"Give me that gun," Bolan said.

"But I thought—"

"I don't trust you," Bolan said flatly. "I don't want you dead, but I don't particularly want you armed and sitting next to me, either."

"Well, you're all heart, man." Baldero frowned. He handed the gun to Bolan, who placed it carefully in his canvas war bag.

"Please tell me that this is over now," the cryptographer said.

"It's not," Bolan said.

"Huh?"

"Do you think they're just magically going to stop tailing us?" Bolan said. "However they've been tracking us, they'll still be doing it. I figure we're due for another visit from our Iranian friends. I don't intend to meet them out in the open or on the road, either."

Baldero looked at the speedometer. "Holy crap, man. Do you know how fast you're going?"

"Not fast enough," Bolan said simply. "Now put on your seat belt."

"You don't have to tell me twice." Baldero shook his head.

Bolan placed a call to the Farm.

"Striker here," he said when Price answered. "Barb, things are coming apart. If Hal's not already up to his neck in bureaucratic quicksand, he soon will be."

"The lights are blinking right across the board, Striker," Price confirmed. "Hal just phoned in with an update, in fact. The Virginia State Police are screaming bloody murder, and we're getting not-so-polite inquiries from the FBI. They want to know why an agent of the Justice Department is running amok in their state."

"I figured it would get worse, once I started leaving bodies behind," Bolan said, then he explained what had just happened.

"It was bad enough when they were random shootings," Price agreed. "But with the current body count, the questions are piling up. Hal's got his network of contacts working with our people in conjunction with the field teams, trying to clean it up and suppress the worst of it, but there's only so much of that they can do. The media are going berserk with it."

"It's going to get worse before I plug these holes," Bolan warned. "Hal understands that, I hope?"

"We all do, Striker," Price said. "I said much the same. He's not happy, but he knows it's necessary for you to do what you do. Just get it done, Striker. We're behind you."

"Good," Bolan said. "There's another complication. I need everything you can get me on an Ayalah Rosen. Possibly Mossad, but definitely linked to Israeli intelligence. The Israelis are in on this somehow, but damned if I can tell you how for sure. Not hard to guess the broad strokes."

"We'll get you the files, Striker."

"All right." He paused. "Barb," he said at last, "I need a location. I'm making pretty good speed, and if I'm really, really lucky we won't have to participate in another running gun battle, but I can't guarantee anything. I need some kind of controlled location, someplace where civilian casualties won't be an issue. Somewhere with some combat room."

"What do you mean?"

"Something like a warehouse, or an abandoned building," Bolan said. "Somewhere urban, but not too populated. A place with options, and enough space to give me room to work. You know the kind of site I need." The Crown Victoria's engine thrummed and vibrated, its power perceptible through the steering wheel. The speedometer was flirting with the far right of the dial as Bolan sped in, around and through traffic. "And while I'm thinking of it, I need you to run interference for me with highway patrol. Keep them off me. I'm still driving the car you sent me."

"We'll work it out for you, Striker," Price said. Bolan heard computer keys clacking and Price conferring with someone, probably Aaron Kurtzman. Then she was back on the line directly. "Striker, can you make it to Richmond?"

"It's a haul. I can sure try."

"We've got something for you. A vacant industrial park in Richmond, not far from the Jefferson Davis Highway. Transmitting directions now."

"Understood. Striker out."

"What are we doing?" Baldero said.

"*We're* not doing anything," Bolan said. "You're going to keep your head down while I try to scratch off some of the fleas."

"What do you mean?"

"The people following you—let's see, there's the Iranians, the French and now, apparently, the Israelis—are going to keep following you. So we're going to get as far ahead of them as we can, then sit down and wait."

"Uh…why?"

"So I can kill them."

"Oh." Baldero was silent for a moment. Then he said, "Hard-core."

"Probably," Bolan said, not taking his eyes from the road.

They drove in silence and at white-knuckle speed. More than once, they saw police vehicles, including state police, but they weren't stopped. Apparently Price had already made good on her promise, as Bolan knew she would. These cops either just weren't interested in the speeding vehicle or, much more likely, they'd been ordered not to interfere.

Eventually the silver Jeep pulled alongside them; Bolan was not surprised. Rosen was in the passenger seat. When the Jeep pulled into the passing lane next to the Crown Victoria, she wrote a phone number, reversed, in lipstick on the glass of her window.

"Holy crap, dude," Baldero said. "She's giving you her number. I think she digs you."

Bolan had nothing to say to that. He snapped open his secure phone and dialed the number, driving with his left hand.

"Mr. Cooper—" Rosen's silken voice was clear over the connection "—it's not nice to rush off before a lady has finished speaking."

"I'm not a particularly nice person," Bolan said frankly. "What do you want?"

"Mr. Cooper, you are driving into something you cannot handle alone. We have been tracking your friend, Mr. Baldero, since he was first acquired by the Iranian death squad you have yourself faced down this day."

"You're not telling me anything I don't know."

"I don't think you realize the scope of this project. By now Mr. Baldero has explained to you the nature of his dilemma, yes?"

"He has." There was no reason he couldn't admit that. She would confirm what he knew, or she wouldn't. Bolan imagined the Israeli woman knew more about the situation than he did.

"Then you know that Mr. Baldero has created, and very foolishly tried to sell on the open market, something very dangerous. A weapon which, in the hands of my country's enemies, would make it very much harder to intercept their plans and preempt their attempts to destroy us."

"I understand that much, yes."

"What you don't know, Mr. Cooper," Rosen went on, "is that a broker, who remains unknown to us, sold Mr. Baldero's encryption program to several very dangerous entities. One was Iran. Another was Liberté dans la Supériorité, known colloquially as the LDLS. It is a French quasi-governmental group that operates with the sanction of the deepest elements within France's military security infrastructure, a sort of secret police to the secret police. Few have heard of it, and certainly the French would not admit it exists. Neither would they acknowledge that the LDLS commits acts of brazen violence in the name of France, to further what they hope to promote as French military superiority around the globe."

"Sounds hard to believe," Bolan said.

"Harder still to cover up as effectively as they do," Rosen said, "for they engage in what would surely be seen as acts of war against even 'friendly' nations. If you capture any of their people, you will discover that any and all are officially dangerous terrorists, wanted for heinous crimes by the French government."

"Will I?"

"You will. But there is more."

"I'm listening."

"In addition to the Iranians and the French," Rosen told him, "we have reason to believe, based on intelligence reports, that North Korea was also contacted, and they, too, may possess the code."

Bolan thought about that. The initial reports had put Asian men with submachine guns at the site of the first shootings.

"Daniel," Bolan said, "describe the men who first shot at you."

"'Daniel'?" Baldero said. "What are we, all friends and crap now? I don't know, man. They were Japanese or something. Maybe Chinese. Definitely Asians."

"And were those same men trying to kill you after that?"

Baldero thought about that. "Well, hell, no, man. I think it was a different bunch. There was an awful damned lot of them—whoever they were. What, are we racially segregating our terrorists now?"

Bolan then said to Rosen, "So it's plausible. What is your point?"

"My point?" The woman sounded amused. "Mr. Cooper, my point is that you're fighting no less than three complete, equipped terrorist forces that have but one goal, and that is to kill the man in your charge."

"I wouldn't call the Iranian complement quite so complete, any longer. Nor the French."

Rosen laughed that musical laugh again. "A fair point. But please, Mr. Cooper, the odds are really too great. I can offer you an alternative."

"And that is?" Bolan began to accelerate. The silver Grand Cherokee moved faster to keep pace. The Israeli driver—Bolan thought it might be Noam, from what little he could see beyond Ayalah's hair blowing in the wind—was good at his job.

"You can give him to us," Rosen said simply. "He is in no danger. We will not kill him. We want only for him to make for us the decryption program. When that is done, he will be set free, once he has been thoroughly debriefed."

"What's she saying?" Baldero asked. He looked suspicious; he could hear just enough of the conversation to wonder.

"No deal," Bolan said.

"But Mr. Cooper," the woman countered, "you know that the assassination squads are tracking Mr. Baldero. We are tracking him as well. We have been monitoring you since you joined him. We were…surprised by your intervention, but I suppose we should not have been. We have our own…I believe you would call them spies—" she said the word playfully "—who have warned us often of the efficacy of America's counterterror and counterintelligence operatives."

"I don't suppose you'd care to tell me *how* you've been tracking this man."

"I cannot, no. Regrettably."

"Forget it," Bolan said. "Baldero stays in the U.S. The decryption program will be made, yes, and I'm sure my government will see to it that its allies receive it."

Rosen swore luridly. Bolan's eyebrows rose at that. "Your government!" she said angrily. "Shall we worry that the next time your presidency changes hands, we will again be told that our settlements are illegitimate, our enemies of no threat to us, our preemptive military strikes illegal, our defensive measures a violation of human rights? No, Mr. Cooper, I do not think I trust the safety and well-being of my people to your government's benevolence! Give us Baldero! Now!"

Bolan hit Mute. He turned to Baldero. "Grab on to something." Then he thumbed the button again. "No deal," he said again.

The connection broke from the other end. Bolan was waiting for the move that came next and responded a fraction of a second quicker. The silver nose of the Jeep suddenly swung their way; Noam was trying to ram them off the road. Bolan, instead of hitting the brake, pressed the accelerator to the firewall. The vehicle shot forward, very nearly spinning its tires despite its already high speed.

The Jeep swerved behind them, going too fast. Bolan again refused to fight it out in traffic; he took the next exit. The Jeep followed, with Noam, now unmistakable behind the wheel as reflected in Bolan's rearview mirror, stuck to the sedan's bumper for all he was worth.

"They're going to ram us," Bolan warned.

"Great," Baldero said.

The nose of the Jeep slammed into the back of the Crown Victoria hard enough to jolt them, but they were both moving so fast that there was no real power behind it. Bolan maneuvered through the curve, listening to the big tires squeal and burn as he pushed to the very edge of their ability to hold the road. The Jeep, with its higher center of gravity, was forced to slow. It was either that or roll over, as both Bolan and, presumably, Noam and his people had witnessed so recently.

They found themselves in a typically commercial district off the exit, dotted with pancake houses, convenience store gas stations and other, similar facilities. Bolan bulled his way into traffic, rudely cutting off other drivers and eliciting a cacophony of honking horns. It didn't take him long to find what he wanted—a quick-oil-change place that was either closed temporarily, or closed for good and therefore vacant. Praying he wouldn't end up diving right into a deep service bay, he gunned the engine and made straight for the closed overhead doors.

"Cooper..." Baldero said. His eyes widened. "Cooper! Cooper!"

Bolan ignored him.

They hit the door.

The segmented and hinged overhead door split into kindling and broken glass when the nose of the vehicle punched through it. Bolan was relieved when they rolled over a metal grate covering the service pit underneath. He motioned for Baldero to get out of the car, throwing open his own door.

The Jeep wasn't far behind. Noam brought the vehicle to a skidding halt, swerving across the bay door opening so that the Grand Cherokee effectively blocked any escape. Bolan moved around to the passenger side of the vehicle, drew the big stainless-steel Desert Eagle from its Kydex sheath and cocked the hammer.

The Israelis piled out of their vehicle. One of them, shouldering a Galil, was somebody Bolan didn't recognize from the rest stop. Apparently Rosen had troops she hadn't yet fully committed, a reserve from which she was drawing—unless the contingent now standing before him was all she had left.

Noam aimed his Glock at Bolan. Rosen, almost reluctantly, brought up her own weapon. Her eyes were hard. She reached out with one hand and made a "gimme" gesture.

Bolan smiled and shook his head.

The man with the Galil took a step forward and snapped the safety of his weapon. It was not a loud sound, but in the sudden silence of the oil change bay, it seemed to echo across the cavernous space. A piece of glass fell free from the shattered bay door and hit the pavement just before the Jeep, shattering into tiny, glittering pebbles.

"You're not taking him," Bolan said. Baldero looked at him, then back to the Israelis.

"You have no choice, Mr. Cooper," Rosen said. "You are out of options."

"No," Bolan said. "I'm not."

The Executioner grabbed Baldero with his left hand, wrapping his arm around the man's throat, and pressed the triangular muzzle of the .44 Magnum Desert Eagle to Baldero's temple.

Roland Collier watched the exchange through his high-powered field glasses and laughed when the big government man put his gun to the CIA cryptographer's head. Hidden in their truck, parked among several similar in the parking lot of a convenience store across the street, he and his team had a perfect view of the little tableau spread before them. What was even more choice, Collier thought, was that the North Koreans were sitting in *their* vehicles not more than a parking lot away, completely oblivious to Collier's presence. The bunch of them thought they were so much smarter than the stupid, fat, lazy Americans, no doubt. Well, Roland Collier thought to himself, he didn't roll over for no chinks, or any Communists either.

He supposed, as he mulled the word over in his mind, that he should avoid using language of that type. Certainly Rafiki, one of the two lieutenants with him, wouldn't take kindly to that kind of thing. Rafiki Hissou despised racism in all its forms, and especially hated whites. He made an exception for Collier and the money Collier paid him, and pretended not to notice the skin color of most of his teammates. As far as Collier was concerned, Rafiki's hypocrisy and his internal conflicts were his business. The coal-black native of the Ivory Coast was a deadly fighter and he knew how to take orders. That's all Collier knew about him, or cared to know.

The third man in the truck was Manfred Skarsgard, a Swedish expatriate. Skarsgard was a deceptively small man who was good with a submachine gun. His hobbies included chess—he and Rafiki often played on a small magnetic travel set Skarsgard carried—and strangling prostitutes. All three of the men were veterans of several campaigns in Africa's war-torn northern states, which was, of course, how Sirus Wassermann had first found them. He had hired them and their comrades on as personal bodyguards and "troubleshooters." Collier liked the term "troubleshooter." It made him think of tough men in similar roles in the movies, and that made him feel good.

Collier reflected, still amused, on the fact that the three of them, alone among all the players on this incredibly busy chessboard, were aware of the scope of the game. The North Koreans thought they knew; they had Tatro at DHS to give them the inside scoop. What that idiot Tatro didn't know was that his supposedly impregnable computer system was infected by a Trojan virus, and that virus was feeding everything he did, saw, received and transmitted to the offices of Sirux-Gibbmann, in a little corner of what had once been part of Liberia and which was currently claimed by the Republic of Côte d'lvoire—what most people knew as the Ivory Coast.

There, Sirus Wassermann, "the eccentric billionaire computer expert," as the papers and magazines always called him, made his headquarters and his fortune. Most of the glowing press reports never mentioned the fact that Wassermann lived in an essentially lawless country because he was wanted for various RICO violations in the United States, not to mention one pesky charge of statutory rape that he couldn't seem to quash. Collier didn't care about any of that, though. Wassermann's money spent like anybody else's, and the crazy old bastard had plenty of it. He also had plenty of need for the services of someone like Collier and his mercenary cohorts, primarily as a private police force and army in Côte d'lvoire. Living where there was no law had its drawbacks, after all. Half a dozen times, Collier or his people had shot down groups of invaders intent on pillaging Sirus's multistory glass-and-steel mansion.

In that respect, Collier was no pawn. He was a much more powerful piece than that. Wassermann needed him, and needed the services he could provide. The old man was also scared to leave his house. He was rumored to be agoraphobic, in fact, and hadn't actually stepped foot on the grounds of his estate in over three years, if the records kept by his house guards were accurate. That meant he needed people like Collier to go out into the world and do his bidding, which made them knights, or rooks, or something. At least.

Collier didn't play chess. It was too complicated a game and far too boring. He liked the way chess metaphors sounded, however, and he used them when he could. If people assumed he was a chess master, well, so much the better. People were impressed by that sort of thing.

Collier had lived most of his professional life, two of the past three decades, trying to impress people. Most of the time, nobody cared, at least not back in the States. He'd tell anybody who would listen that he'd been Force Recon in the Marines, twice decorated, and so what if maybe that wasn't *strictly* true? He'd enrolled, hadn't he? If he hadn't gotten hurt in basic training he'd have gone on to do great things, and hell, he'd studied multiple martial arts and earned black belts in them. He was one tough mother, and he had a tattoo on his right bicep that said so. He'd actually done pretty well at judo in his day. Of course, that story changed a bit in the retelling, and he saw no shame in embellishing a little bit. He was just giving proper warning when he told people he'd spent some time on the illegal pit-fighting circuit, back when he was living on the streets in his late teenager years. He'd earned his living, he would tell people, fighting in parking lots at night in illegal bare-knuckle brawls. He could almost picture it—the ring of headlights from the circle of parked cars, the screams of the crowd, the feeling of blood on his knuckles…

None of that had ever happened, really, but it could have. In reality, Collier had made his bones in and out of reform schools and jails back in the States, before he finally responded to an advertisement in the back of a soldiering magazine and hopped a plane to Northern Africa. There, he had done some fighting and even some honest-to-God close protective work. He'd learned that he was very, very good at one thing, something that surprised even him, and he took pride in having a real, marketable skill.

Roland Collier was hell on wheels at following people.

He had a natural talent for tailing. The other mercenaries he worked with, fighting in the urban slums of Northern Africa's most strife-torn countries, such as Liberia, Burkina Faso and the Ivory Coast, had nicknamed him "Tailgunner," even though it did not, strictly speaking, make sense. Collier didn't care. He'd fought all his life for that kind of respect. If maybe they were making fun of him sometimes when they said it, fine. He had eventually fought his way into the good graces of Wassermann, which meant *he* was in charge finally, damn it.

His talent for tailing had served him very, very well on this mission, which was why he had told Wassermann so confidently that he would take the assignment and that he could succeed at it. He and the other mercs working with him had been pulling guard duty for weeks at the Sirux-Gibbmann building, doing little more than standing around checking and rechecking their weapons, talking about girls they claimed they'd laid and making up stories about fights they'd been in. At least, that was how Collier spent his time; he had no reason to think his fellow soldiers-for-hire were any different in that way. Their pockets would fill up every pay day, they'd take the trucks in shifts into town to visit the whores there and drink the lousy booze in the shanty-town bars, and then they'd come back, hung over and full of themselves, until the next pay period rolled around. It wasn't a bad life, Collier figured.

Then, surprise, surprise, he'd gotten the summons from Wassermann through one of the man's servants. They hadn't even seen Wassermann around the building for weeks. Sometimes, very rarely, he'd pass through the halls, a stoop-shouldered scarecrow of a sixty-year-old, wearing tweed pants and an old sweater, a pair of wire-rimmed spectacles perched on his forehead as if he'd forgotten them. When he was told that his employer wanted a word with him directly, Collier had been absolutely shocked. He'd gone, as much out of curiosity as anything else. At the time he'd been a little worried that the gravy train was over, and that he and his "coworkers," as Wassermann insisted on calling them, would need to trade their cushy assignment for one in which people were shooting at them again.

In Collier's limited experience and opinion, Africans couldn't shoot for shit, but that didn't mean they couldn't get lucky once in a while. He was not eager to get back into the middle of a hot brush war, nor did he want to help some would-be warlord control three square blocks of crumbling North African ghetto.

He shouldn't have worried about it, looking back. Wassermann's butler ushered him into the man's inner office. It was a creepy, dimly-lighted room dominated by a large, round desk. Empty soda cans and half-full bags of snack food littered those portions of the desk not devoted to electronic equipment, memory cards, or stacks of CDs in and out of jewel cases. At least two dozen flat-screen monitors and multiple keyboards were arrayed on racks around the desk in a half circle. Cables ran everywhere. The heat from the machines humming away under the big, round desk was dispelled by a wall-mounted, ductless air-conditioning unit that churned away at full power, spraying the room's nearly constant occupant with a drifting, misty cloud of cool vapor.

At the center of all this, crouched like a spider suspended uncomfortably in the middle of a poorly spun web, sat Wassermann. He looked hunched and red-eyed, his face a shadowy skull in the glow of the monitors before him. He did not look away from the screens when he spoke. His voice was a rasping croak, and the entire time he was speaking, his fingers were crabbing across the keys faster than Collier would have thought possible. The click-click-clack of the keyboards he played, a silent virtuoso on his chosen instrument, never stopped. Collier had no way to know what the man was doing. Writing code? Carrying on conversations? Demanding sexual acts from web-streamed performers in pornographic chat rooms? Whatever he was doing, his hands seemed disconnected from the rest of him, as if he were possessed. Wassermann made Collier very uncomfortable. He smelled of decay, as if he was dying from some disease.

It had been a very odd conversation. It wasn't a conversation at all, Collier had to admit. Wassermann had done all the talking, and Collier had merely nodded or said, "Yes, sir" when it was expected of him. He had of course agreed to the mission. Wassermann was willing to throw an ungodly amount of money in his direction. He wasn't about to say no to that.

Wassermann had droned on for a while, telling Collier things he already knew—that Sirux-Gibbmann Enterprises was one of the world's leading marketers of encryption software, serving civilian and military markets around the world; that Wassermann made it is his business to stay on top of developments in privacy software and cryptography on multiple fronts; that Sirux-Gibbmann was known for its predatory business practices. While he was surprised that Wassermann would admit openly to the negative opinions held about him and his company, even mentioning, in passing, the charges that had forced him to leave the United States some years ago, Collier wasn't learning anything new. Then Wassermann's expression had changed.

Sounding conspiratorial, Wassermann had leaned forward—though never taking his eyes from his precious monitors, his fingers typing away the whole time—and said, quietly, that he occupied a number of online discussion sites devoted to programming and advanced coding topics. On these sites he routinely monitored the questions and progress of those in his field who might, one day, prove to be able employees—or dangerous competitors. One such young man, it seemed, had caught his eye, a man whose ideas about code were truly revolutionary, whose grasp of what Wassermann called "fuzzy logic heuristics" was almost equal to Wassermann's own.

Using his knowledge of computer networks, it had been easy for Wassermann to track down the supposedly anonymous poster. He had worked up a complete dossier on the man, this Daniel Baldero. He had even managed to break into Baldero's home network and make a copy of the earliest version of the encryption program the man had designed. With modifications of Wasserman's own, that program was slated to go on sale next year as Sirux-Gibbmann's latest offering in the competitive commercial encryption and firewall market.

The only problem was, of course, that Baldero could ruin it all if he wasn't, as Wassermann put it, *contained*.

According to Wassermann, there was little about Baldero's life that he did not know, and that included all of the private communications between Baldero and an "anonymous" agent of the Department of Homeland Security. Thus Wassermann knew more about the cryptographer's business deal than Baldero himself. From the center of his web, Wassermann had plucked the strands necessary to follow back to their sources all of the data trails both men were leaving.

Baldero, bless his naive heart, had apparently thought he was selling his code to somebody who could middleman it to friendly nations only. Apparently he hadn't figured on the profit motive of Tatro, who was as corrupt as they came. The most profits were to be had from rogue nations, and that's exactly where he'd shopped Baldero's final version of the encryption program.

The Iranians, the French and the North Koreans, all understood just what they had, and they started throwing money at Tatro for his help in eliminating or capturing the source of the code. Apparently Tatro had asked Baldero for the decryption code, and Baldero had told him it did not, as yet, exist—that the decryption heuristics would take him twice as long as the original encryption coding. He'd have to wait, Baldero had told him, before they could make any money selling clients the ability to crack the uncrackable code. Tatro had turned around and gleefully sold this information to his list of shady customers. The result was the current dueling armies of foreign nationals gunning for Baldero on American soil.

Somewhere along the way, the Israelis had gotten into the act, probably because, in Wassermann's thinking, they were already monitoring the Iranians, at the very least. They were easily smarter than the others, and chances were good it was from the Israelis that Collier and his men would eventually steal Baldero…but of course they'd have to see about that. There were an awful lot of enemy trigger-pullers between there and here.

The DHS man had really made it easy for the bastards, too, though so far Baldero and that American agent had proved too cagey for them. Tatro had given the North Koreans, the Iranians and the French some kind of tracking device—something they were using to home in on Baldero time and time again. The Israelis had either acquired a similar device, or through their intelligence sources they'd built one of their own. It didn't matter how; they were following along with all the others, and it had been all Collier could do not to accidentally stumble onto the crazy train of hunters and killers who were trooping after Baldero.

Wassermann did not himself have access to that tracking device or information on it, which was not kept in any of the computer networks he had penetrated to that point, but it didn't matter. From Tatro's own files, he knew precisely with whom the agent had been dealing. He knew how they were scheduled to get into the country. He had copies of the forged diplomatic documents that would permit those deadly assassination teams to cross American borders, their cargoes of small arms and explosives unsearched. In short, he knew everything he needed to know to put a very crafty Collier on the trail of the groups who were in turn pursuing Baldero.

The idea was to hang back until it was clear who the winning party would be and then take Baldero from them. Wassermann had it in his head that he could entice Baldero to work for him, so he wanted the man alive. When Collier broke his chain of "Yes, sirs" to ask why Wassermann didn't simply offer Baldero a job in the first place, the old man had been dismissive. He had said simply that he didn't want there to be any possibility Baldero could say no. Collier figured he understood that.

Getting back into the country had been easy, thanks to the documents Wassermann had forged for them. He could reach out and stick his fingers into practically any computer in the world. It wasn't unthinkable that, while he'd been snooping around in Tatro's computer, he'd taken the DHS man's files and used the same package of forged credentials that had gotten the other terrorists into the U.S.A. Collier, his lieutenants and the other mercenaries they'd brought with them all carried forged travel visas and faked driver's licenses. They probably wouldn't hold up to detailed scrutiny, but Collier didn't intend to let things get that far. They would just wait for somebody to get Baldero. Then they'd steal him. If any cops got in their way…well, Collier hated cops. He'd hated them since his brushes with the law had finally forced him to leave the country. He'd been staring down the barrel of a few years in prison, in fact, for a charge of battery on a police officer.

He snorted at that. Battery on a police officer. His ass. Those cops had been battering on *him* pretty damned good before somebody had stopped them, and just because he'd socked one of the arrogant bastards in the jaw…

It no longer mattered, he thought. Nobody here knew about that, anyway. His West Virginia drawl was not too out of place here in Virginia, but Rafiki and Skarsgard didn't know he'd been born and raised not very far from this spot, and he wasn't about to tell them. Who knew? Maybe they even believed his many stories about his life on the street and his time in the Marines. As long as they knew not to mess with him, that was all that mattered. Collier was one tough mother, and they would do well to remember that. Once he'd collected the pay for this job, he intended to live the high life for a while, spending Wassermann's money and telling stories about the men he'd fought, hand-to-hand, during his most recent, daring commando raid in the United States. What a bunch of whores didn't know wouldn't hurt them any.

In the silent scene played out in his binoculars, the big American had apparently bluffed his way past the Israelis. He was backing into his cop's car and pulling out, slowly, as one of the Israelis pulled their Jeep out of the way. The whole time, the big guy had that pimp-looking miniature cannon he toted jammed in the side of Baldero's head. The Israelis weren't looking to push the issue, apparently, at least not here. The hot broad in charge of them looked plenty mad, too, and that made Collier smile. He had no use for uppity women who were too pretty for their own good. Maybe he'd have a chance to show her what he thought before this was over.

He shook the thought away. There would be time for that later. He licked his lips.

There was *always* time for that kind of thing.

10

"You're freaking kidding me, right?" Baldero asked hotly as the Crown Victoria rolled up the entrance ramp and began to pick up speed on the highway. "A gun to my effing head?"

"Would you have rather gone with Ayalah and her people?" Bolan asked. "I guarantee their idea of persuading you would be unpleasant. You might not survive it."

"You put a gun to my head!"

"Calm down," Bolan said without taking his eyes from the road. "I wouldn't have shot you."

"You wouldn't have… Then why do it, if you wouldn't have shot me?"

"Well, they didn't know that."

Baldero just stared at him. Finally, he slumped into his seat, crossed his arms and swore under his breath.

"Put your seat belt on," Bolan told him.

The trip to Richmond, on Highway 64 back the way Bolan and Baldero had traveled separately to Norfolk, was quiet. Baldero sat in sullen silence while the soldier drove. The sedan's engine screamed as Bolan pushed it as hard as he could, determined to gain as much advantage in distance and time as he could make. His plan hinged on them getting to Richmond and to the location identified for him by Stony Man. Given just how badly they had managed to hurt the Iranians and the French that morning, chances were very good they could pull it off. He had no illusions that the enemy would not regroup and pursue again, for they had done so repeatedly, but there was no doubt that he had hurt them. He had hurt them badly, in fact. Their forces, while large, were finite, and operating on what was for them a non-permissive environment fraught with risks of discovery.

That meant, Bolan knew, that while he could speed past everything else on the highway, traveling on the shoulder when necessary and moving in and out of the traffic that appeared to be standing still by comparison, his pursuers would need to remain relatively legal. They could not risk being pulled over for speeding and, frankly, Bolan hoped if they did speed, no one happened to stop them. He did not like the thought of some state trooper walking into that mess unaware. If it had been in his power to prevent such a scenario, he would gladly have taken on more risk to himself to do so.

He was within just a few miles of Richmond when he saw yet another police car. This one ignored him, as had all the others. Price and Stony Man were still covering him, unseen but always there when he required their assistance.

Baldero was looking around with interest, apparently having worked out to his own satisfaction that Bolan had not intended to put a bullet in his brain.

That had been a tense moment, but there was no other way. The Israelis needed Baldero alive. They knew Bolan would at least theoretically want Baldero alive, too, but they'd also seen him shoot down, on his own, countless armed men that morning. He had ruthlessly bludgeoned Noam when it had been necessary to do so. They would not know just how far he was willing to go and, therefore, they could not risk Baldero's life gambling that Bolan's move was a bluff. They had also not been willing to murder Bolan to get the cryptographer—which had been a complete gamble on the soldier's part. He had not been entirely certain of their limitations in that regard. They could very well simply have shot him to take Baldero away.

In the end, the standoff had gotten him what he wanted: The Israelis had reluctantly allowed him to leave, Ayalah Rosen vowing that this was, in fact, not over. Bolan did not doubt her.

During the trip to Richmond, the Farm had called him with updated information on Rosen. She was—according to the dossier Price transmitted to him and from which she read over the phone—known to be working with or for a splinter group of radical Israelis, who were trying hard to establish a shadow government under Israel's legitimate government. The Israelis had known about the problem for some time, but either Rosen's group, which had no name, at least none known to U.S. intelligence sources, enjoyed furtive sanction from the powers that were in Israel, or it was too powerful for the official government to root out and eradicate.

In either case, Rosen and her operatives were former Mossad, at least nominally wanted by the government of Israel for various and sundry crimes. The official files, Price warned Bolan, noted that Rosen and her top people were likely still drawing on government and military contacts both in their country and in countries around the world. That accounted for how they had penetrated the United States, at least in Bolan's mind, and it also explained how they had managed to learn so much about the existence of Baldero's encryption program and the efforts of the Iranians and rogue French operatives to acquire or assassinate the program's author.

Before the soldier signed off, Price told him that Brognola was pursuing, through the Justice Department, several lines of inquiry into what appeared to be the worst breach of U.S. border security on record. The big Fed was apparently overloading the phone lines between Justice and State, when he wasn't continuing to shield Bolan from the legal fallout and jurisdictional bitching that always resulted when the Executioner waged one of his personal battle campaigns on American soil. That was the extent of what Brognola could do to cover Bolan on this mission, but that, the soldier reflected, would be more than enough. The rest was up to the Executioner.

The GPS application in his secure sat phone led him directly to the warehouse location the Farm had selected according to his requirements. He was pleased to see that, while the rest of the immediate area was relatively busy, the warehouse complex itself was deserted, with large No Trespassing signs and chain barriers delineating the property. He accelerated through one of these. The Crown Victoria's somewhat abused grille made short work of it. Bolan could hear the end of the snapped chain take a long gouge out of the side of the car's paint job as it whipped past.

"I've always wanted to do that," Baldero said.

Bolan ignored him. He drove toward the largest of the warehouse buildings, which appeared to be a two-story, tiered affair that might offer more than just a large, square space. Cover and concealment he would have to improvise.

He stopped the Crown Victoria at the large double doors on the south end of the warehouse complex. These were large enough to permit a tractor trailer, or perhaps even two abreast, to pass into the building. He got out, warning Baldero to stay where he was, and checked the padlock securing the door.

It was a big model of the type used to secure trailer doors in transit. He stepped back a few paces, drew the .44 Magnum Desert Eagle and aimed carefully.

The big gun boomed and its triangular muzzle rocked up slightly as he rode out the familiar recoil. The lock was blasted into pieces, and a fragment ricocheted from his shin, stinging him. Bolan paid that no mind. In battle he incurred any number of small scrapes, bruises, cuts and punctures; this was little more than a reminder that his nerve endings were still firing normally despite much battlefield abuse.

The interior of the warehouse looked quite promising. The upper level wasn't a full floor at all, but an enclosed catwalk, of sorts, running the perimeter of the second level and providing an overhang of the ground floor. There were windows up there that would be natural points of tactical superiority for an invading force, and thus would prove very tempting.

On the ground level, there were pits recessed in the far end. These were long, low grooves the size of trailers, which were designed to put the floor of a truck's trailer on a level even with the concrete floor of the warehouse. Bolan checked the access doors at that end and found them bolted shut, not just padlocked, which was to his advantage. He returned to the vehicle and pulled the Crown Victoria back, parking it in the center of the warehouse floor.

"Uh…isn't this kind of exposed?" Baldero asked.

"That's the idea," Bolan said.

"I am *not* waiting in the car," Baldero said firmly.

"No, you're not." Bolan pointed to the second level. "You're going to help me carry some things to the second floor. Then you're going to get yourself into the farthest of those truck pits and stay there."

"I heard that," Baldero said. "Cooper?"

"Yeah."

"Why do you do it?"

"Do what?"

"You know. This. Risk your ass. Get shot at. Kill twenty men before breakfast. All this crap."

Bolan eyed him. "Because this nation is worth fighting for," Bolan said. "Because its people are worth fighting for. Because they can't all fight for themselves, and I can."

"So somebody's got to?"

"Something like that."

"So why don't you, I don't know," Baldero said, "call in

the Marines or something? Air support? Cobra gunships, a platoon to back you up? You got connections, right?"

"No way they could get here in time," Bolan said. "Not as razor-thin as our margin is. Until we know how they're tracking you, Daniel, there's no way we could put that in place. But we can manage the next best thing."

Bolan popped the trunk of the Crown Victoria and surveyed its contents. *Be sure to check inside the trunk,* Price had said. He'd known what she was referring to just as she said it. Kissinger knew exactly the type of thing Bolan was likely to need on a job like this, and he would have made sure the vehicle the Farm arranged for him to pick up was properly packed. It was.

Baldero uttered a particularly blasphemous curse. "Is that...?" he started. "Are those...?"

The heavy plastic crate in the trunk contained several rows of olive-drab, slightly curved bricks. Bolan picked up one of them. The words "FRONT TOWARD ENEMY" were raised in its surface. A small black box with an LED on it was wired to the back of each one, near the top. Bolan would not have dared to use heavy ordnance on the road, where the likelihood of innocent civilians in the crossfire dictated his run-and-gun tactics. But with room to work and a fixed location from which to operate, he could finally use some of the assortment of high-explosive goodies with which the Farm had provided him.

The devices were Claymore mines, modified M-18 A-1 antipersonnel devices converted to electronic detonation by Kissinger. Each mine was a green plastic housing bearing a pair of metal scissors-legs. Inside each one, a shaped layer of C-4 plastic explosive sat under a matrix of hundreds of steel balls the size of birdshot.

"LAW rockets?" Baldero asked, picking up one of the short metal tubes that also sat in the trunk. "You've actually got LAW rockets?"

"Give me that," Bolan said absently, taking the launcher from Baldero. He gathered up a couple of the other launchers. The M-72 Light Antitank Weapon was something he had used many, many times. Each one was a lightweight, self-contained antiarmor weapon effective to perhaps 200 meters. Each single-use LAW tube carried a fin-stabilized rocket that in turn bore a 66 mm High Explosive Anti Tank—HEAT—warhead.

"On second thought, help me with those." Bolan jerked his chin toward the rockets that remained. Baldero helped him carry the weapons to one of the truck pits, where Bolan arranged them in the corner for ready access. There was a series of steps at the end of the pit on which he could stand, to give him enough height to sight over—and shoot over—the edge of the pit.

Bolan glanced at the Marathon TSAR diver's watch he wore on his left wrist. They had been here long enough that the numbers were starting to fall critically; as close as Baldero's pursuers had followed thus far, they would be here soon. He was actually mildly surprised they hadn't come already, but he wasn't going to complain about good fortune breaking his way. Sometimes, in combat, luck was all you had—luck, and will.

He dug into his canvas war bag and produced the Glock pistol he had taken from the Israelis earlier. He press-checked it, probably unnecessarily, knowing that whenever a gun had been out of his direct sight, he would not take its condition for granted. Then he handed the gun butt-first to Baldero.

"Take this," he said. "Get into the farthest pit."

"What about the second floor?"

"Let me worry about that," Bolan said. "I don't like our odds."

Baldero nodded. He understood, finally, what Bolan was about to do. "Listen, Cooper," he said, "thank you for…well, for looking out for me. You're risking your life for me, and I don't want you to think I don't know it."

"I'm not," Bolan said. He gathered up the crate of Claymores in both hands, after first pocketing the remote detonator clipped to its side. "I'm doing it for you, and for everyone else."

"Because somebody's got to?" Baldero asked, only slightly sarcastic.

"Yeah," Bolan said. "Now get down there."

"Yes sir, Mr. Cooper, sir," Baldero said, throwing Bolan a cocky salute.

Bolan ignored him.

Moving quickly, the Executioner began to leave his deadly toys at strategic points throughout the warehouse. He found a ladder enclosed in a cylinder of protective steel cagework. He climbed it to the upper level and began placing his mines, paying special attention to the windows spaced evenly along the length of the outer roof.

When he was done, he had four mines left. He knew just where he wanted to put them, and did so. As he was extending the scissors feet of the last explosive package and making sure the LED on its electronic detonator was glowing amber, he heard vehicles outside the building.

The enemy was here, right on schedule.

Bolan hurried to the truck pit in which he had staged the LAW rockets. As he jumped in, throwing a last glance at the far pit where Baldero was hiding, he heard gunfire.

The answering automatic fire, different in timbre and clearly fired from a different vantage, took him by surprise. It was quickly apparent that a firefight was raging outside the building that did not involve him.

The French and Iranians had discovered each other, it seemed.

He waited, his combat reflexes humming, his senses heightened as they always were when battle came to him or when he brought it to others.

The wooden doors at the opposite end of the warehouse

weren't locked, but the cargo van that smashed through them came hurtling through the barrier in a storm of broken wood nonetheless. The first van was followed by another, and if they were still using the same transportation, this would be the Iranians.

Over the engines of the invaders and the crashing of pieces of the warehouse doors, Bolan heard glass breaking on the level above. The Iranians, or perhaps the French, were taking the obvious route into the building from above. They had either found roof access outside—Bolan had not bothered to scout for that, assuming they would find a way if they were inclined to do it—or they had done it the hard way, scaling the outside of the building with rope and grappling hooks, or whatever equivalent tool they might have at hand.

Bolan counted off the numbers in his head, still protected in the truck pit, listening as the vans screeched to sliding, rubber-burning halts on the concrete floor above and beyond him. He counted one, then two, and finally three seconds. Then he thumbed a combination of buttons on the digital detonator Kissinger had provided.

The staccato explosions sounded like the rolling of thunder in the enclosed roof space of the warehouse. They came one after another, not quite staggered, overlapping each and the next in a symphony of high-explosive carnage. Bolan could not see what was happening, but he didn't need to. He had observed the use, and the bloody aftermath, of the Claymore mines before. The shaped charges would hurl the lethal, vicious swarms of steel balls in the direction the shaped C-4 charge hurled them, scything through anything that stood or knelt in their path. They would deal instant death at close range, a horrible, lingering death several feet farther out and, for the very unlucky among the invaders, an interminable suffering that would at the very least put the enemy gunners out of action with shredded limbs or debilitating flesh wounds.

Bolan had created a charnel house, a shotgun cross fire of whirling, spinning, high-speed fatality.

Bolan, his blood cool, his nerves completely calm while hell erupted about him, turned to the small stack of LAW rockets. He picked up one of them.

The soldier rotated the rear cover of the rocket tube, allowing the front cover and sling assembly to fall free. He yanked the pull pin, discarding the front cover and the sling. Then he grabbed both ends of the rocket tube and pulled, extending the LAW to its firing length.

He shouldered the weapon and sighted on the nearer cargo van, even as the chaos on the upper level rained shrapnel, glass, wood and body parts in all directions. Then he snapped the arming handle into position, took a firm grip on the rubber boot over the trigger bar and drew in a breath.

The Executioner expelled half the breath and then held it.

He fired.

The antitank rocket blew the cargo van to metal slivers. The explosion blossomed in an overwhelming burst of blistering heat, blinding light and deafening sound, tossing about the Iranian shooters by the vehicle like paper dolls in a wind tunnel. Bolan dropped the empty rocket tube, readied another one and aimed again, this time targeting the second van. The Iranian gunners, identifiable by their home-produced bullpup rifles, were running for their lives, confusion and even terror evident on their fitfully flame-lighted faces.

Several men ran for Bolan's Crown Victoria, parked temptingly in the center of the concrete expanse. The Executioner saw them going for it, ducked again still unseen and tapped another sequence on the detonator.

The Claymore mines positioned in the side pockets of the sedan's doors were oriented toward the interior of the car. When Bolan set them off, the doors were open. The Iranians probably hoped to take the vehicle and drive it, quickly, to safety through the exploding mess tearing the building apart. What they got, instead, were explosions of their own, as hundreds of steel spheres burst outward and shredded their bodies at close range.

Suddenly grenades started to bounce and roll through the warehouse. These were not Bolan's. He couldn't tell from where they had come, but the first one that exploded blew the back of the Crown Victoria to flaming cinders, igniting the gas tank and shoving the entire car up and sideways. It came back down on burning tires, little more than a scorched frame from the rear seats back.

The thumps of the fragmentation grenades—their sounds, too, very familiar to Bolan's combat-trained ears—ripped through the space. Automatic gunfire, sporadic at first, began to sound from the catwalk on the upper level. Bolan, from his angle, caught a glimpse of M-16 barrels and at least one Colt SMG. Empty shell casings rained down from above.

It was time to redouble the chaos.

Bolan fished out all of his remaining smoke canisters from the canvas war bag. He began pulling the pins and, while the battle raged on the levels above, started throwing them into the warehouse space from his location in the truck pit.

The grenades popped and hissed as they began spewing their thick, colored smoke. Plumes of purple, blue and yellow vapor began to spread across the interior of the warehouse hellscape, the noxious fumes choking the men running about within them who found themselves suddenly unable to see to target their weapons.

It was time to join the battle directly.

Bolan made sure the spare, loaded magazines for his mini-Uzi were at hand in the side pockets of his canvas war bag. Checking the fit of the wide strap over his shoulder, he cocked the submachine gun. His Beretta and the Desert Eagle were in their usual places on his body, practically a part of him. The spare magazines for these were on his person and also filling out the shoulder bag. He was ready for anything and prepared to deal the enemy a serious blow.

He was rigged for war.

Bolan climbed out of the pit with the mini-Uzi in his fist,

emerging from the pall of smoke like an avenging god. The enemy was in complete disarray. Shooters were running back and forth through the chaos, desperate to find a cover, to find an exit…it was impossible to say which. The gunfire continued from the upper level, but it was unfocused and fairly ineffective. Whoever was left alive up there couldn't see through the smoke any more than could the men below. The shooters were hitting one another, and whether their targets were members of the opposing kill team or friendly members of their own side was no more clear to them than it was to Bolan.

The Executioner had the advantage in this maelstrom of death and confusion, for there were no friendlies here. There were only those trying to take Baldero for their own purposes, and the cryptographer himself, safely tucked away out of the line of fire. It didn't matter where Bolan's bullets flew in this enclosed killing field, this target-rich artificial environment of his own making.

The Executioner did what he did best.

He stalked through the carnage, his combat boots crushing spent shell casings underfoot, taking it slow as he made his way through the smoke, feeling his way around the hot spots from the burning vehicles. He had blown all of the Claymores; there were no other large vehicles for his LAW rockets to seek. Finally it was just Bolan and whatever remained of the enemies, as it invariably came down to when he entered the fray.

A man emerged from the smoke, firing an Iranian bullpup rifle in Bolan's general direction. The soldier squeezed off a burst that ripped up the man's sternum before he fell down dead.

The gunfire seemed to draw the attention of the gunners in the immediate area, while the muzzle-flashes gave the men on the upper level something to target. Bullets began to spall and whine off the concrete, raising stony shrapnel that was almost as dangerous as the gunfire itself. Bolan ignored it. Squinting against the haze he had created, he half crouched and leaned into his shots, holding the mini-Uzi with both hands and bracing its unfolded metal bar stock against his shoulder.

An enemy appeared; he burned the man down. Another fired at him. He fired a shot that cored through the man's eye and dropped him neatly in place. He shot another, and another, and another. The gunfire was closing on his position, ripping the floor near his booted feet, but he could not acknowledge it. He emptied the Uzi with one long, last burst, mowing down the ranks of the enemy shooters as fast as they could come.

He swapped the spent magazine for a fresh one, then he was walking, firing, walking again, moving back and forth in a random pattern, ducking, weaving, slipping, bobbing... always firing, always moving, emptying the magazine as he had the one before it.

Every part of the Executioner was alive as he moved through the kill zone. A man with a pistol drew down on him; Bolan sprayed the Uzi laterally and took him apart with a blast across his neck. He let the Uzi continue traveling, its recoil dragging the muzzle forward as he canted it on its side. In less time than it would take to describe, Bolan had killed another trio of men, bunched together with the lead shooter whom Bolan had practically decapitated.

He kept on burning the warehouse clean, ridding it of the predators who had so eagerly invaded it. He changed magazines in the mini-Uzi, and then again, and again, and kept on using them and burning through them. He did not lose count—he almost never lost count. But then the Uzi was empty, its muzzle burning hot, and he dropped it back in his shoulder bag as he drew the .44 Magnum Desert Eagle.

He saw them, then, recognizing the man from the dossiers the Farm had transmitted to him. One of the Iranians, Marzieh Shirazi, covered in blood and looking more like a walking skeleton than a man, was strangling another man, unidentifiable in civilian clothes. The man Shirazi was strangling still held the pistol grip of an AR-15-pattern assault rifle, but his finger was not on the trigger and it was clear he was either unconscious or dead. The Iranian terrorist, Shirazi, spotted Bolan through the smoke and fire and surged to his feet.

Bolan tracked left with the Desert Eagle. As Shirazi charged, he extended his gnarled hands like claws, an inhuman sound escaping his lips.

The soldier fired.

The Desert Eagle thundered once, then again, then a third time, and then Shirazi was on top of him, incredibly, surprisingly strong, knocking him onto his back. Bolan took the fall across his shoulders as best he could, grunting with the impact and tucking his head to prevent a concussion. Then Shirazi had his hands around the soldier's throat.

As he went down, Bolan had drawn the Desert Eagle back, holding it cross against his body at an angle, a proved method for shooting from retention. He fired, feeling the muzzle-blast scorch his abdomen. He pulled the trigger until the big weapon was empty, trying to blow Shirazi off him.

Incredibly, the terrorist took every slug and did not fall. His face turned a livid shade of purple, and the man squeezed Bolan's neck with all his might. The soldier felt his vision starting to blur, then to gray at the edges, as the Iranian began literally to squeeze the life out of him.

Bolan clubbed the man with the empty Desert Eagle, while prying at the viselike fingers with his left hand. He struck Shirazi in the side of the head with a brutal blow. Something cracked and the Iranian's eyes began to roll up into his head.

The Executioner could breathe again. He bucked and threw the bloody terrorist off him. The body slumped to the concrete floor limply, a puppet with its strings cut. Bolan surveyed the number of wounds the man had sustained, not all of them bullet holes of his own making. He had seen it before, of course. In battle, with adrenaline coursing through their bodies and a murderous fever beginning to grip them, many men went completely berserk, evoking the crazed warriors of ages past. Shirazi had been dead perhaps even before Bolan shot him; he would have succumbed from his wounds eventually. He had gone on to fight like a demon even after the repeatedly fatal shots the soldier had dealt him. It was a sobering thought.

He spared the dead Iranian a final glance and then was on the move again, for he had no time to further consider the corpse. The smoke was beginning to clear. In the flickering light of the burning vans and his own wrecked Crown Victoria, he could see only a few more figures moving at this level.

He reloaded the Desert Eagle, then fell to one knee, risking remaining stationary, temporarily, for the stability it offered him as a shooting platform. Bracing the big weapon with both hands, he took careful aim through what was left of the wisps of smoke.

He identified his targets as they came. Each one was armed. Each was clearly a member of the invading forces—Bolan would never gun down a person unless he was sure of just who or what he was shooting. As he acquired his targets, he swiveled on his knee and pressed the big handgun's trigger.

Each man's head was snapped back as a 240-grain jacketed hollowpoint round blasted through it. One by one the corpses collapsed limply to the floor. Every enemy that fell away meant one less between the Executioner and victory over the small army arrayed against him.

As he cleared the lower level, he was moving toward the caged ladder leading to the catwalk. Once he reached it, he holstered the Desert Eagle and drew his Beretta 93-R.

Using one hand and bracing his back against the enclosing cage to stay on the ladder, Bolan made his way up. As he emerged on the catwalk, a bullet ricocheted noisily from the uppermost rung of the ladder. The soldier dropped back, stopping himself before he could slide down more than a few rungs. He reached up with one leg, gathered himself and then jumped back up.

It was a close call. Several rounds almost took him in the chest, and would have, if he had not pulled himself up with desperate speed and rolled out of the cage and onto the catwalk. As it was, he felt a round crease his ribs. He couldn't think about that—all his thoughts remained focused on getting clear and acquiring this new threat.

He shoved the 93-R to full extension from the ground, tracking and firing, punching a 3-round burst into the gunner's chest.

Up and on the move again, he surveyed the incredible destruction that had been wrought on the catwalk by his strategically placed Claymores. There were dead men everywhere. He saw several rappelling lines coiled and ready, some spilled across the catwalk and dangling down. All the outer windows were broken out, if not by the invaders, then by the mines he had detonated.

The spherical shot in the mines had done its deadly work over and over again, shredding all resistance and making an abattoir of the upper level. Bolan moved across the metal and wooden deck-work, careful to watch his footing. The catwalk was slick with blood and littered with everything from shell casings to wood splinters to pieces of the enemy shooters. The air was thick with the smells of death, the smoke canisters, the burning vehicles…and possibly an insulation fire. He looked around carefully, spotting a few areas within the walls that appeared to be burning freely. He paused to kick at these with his boots, stomping them out. It would not do to have the entire building go up, or spread to the warehouses on either side of it.

Amid the wreckage, both material and human, Bolan picked

his way along the catwalk. A fallen man stirred, then shrieked horribly. The soldier took one look at him and, while he did not turn away—if you can shoot a man, you ought to be able to look at what you've done, Bolan had always thought—he immediately knew that there was nothing that could be done for the fallen gunman. The Claymores had done their cruel work only too well. He unleathered the Beretta and fired a quick mercy round.

He continued on, checking the entire circuit of the catwalk. He found only one other man still alive. As Bolan neared, the man muttered something.

"Ne me tuez pas..." the man murmured. *"...suis sans armes..."*

Bolan stood over the gravely wounded man. The Claymores had torn him up. He was clutching something in his hand. The soldier bent and gently pried the device from the man's bloody fingers.

It was roughly the size of a PDA and was blank except for a number pad. A steel ball from one of the mines had shattered its screen badly, but it was still working, after a fashion. A glowing amber blip on the screen corresponded roughly with Baldero's position, down in the truck pit.

He took a good look at the man's face and thought it was familiar. Setting the tracker aside, he opened his phone, scanning through the dossier thumbnails the Farm had transmitted. He found a match and brought up the file.

The man was, according to the Farm's data, a known associate of several of the dead French terrorists Bolan had snapped after his first engagement with what he could only describe, in the context of this mission, as the French hit team.

His name: Dominique Uhlan. He was, according to the data files, known to be at least a sometime member of Liberté dans la Supériorité. Ayalah Rosen's intel was good, it seemed. He would have to thank her when he saw her again—though he truly hoped he did not. It was relief enough to know that Rosen and her Israeli splinter group were not among the shooters in the warehouse. Had they tried to take Baldero by force, he would have shot them down as readily as he did these other killers, but it would not have been the same thing. Killing these terrorists, these would-be assassins or kidnappers, was an act of justice, even of retribution, for they represented the types of predators who were even at this moment doing their best to burn down the civilized world.

Ayalah Rosen and her radicals were misguided, by comparison. If they threatened the security of the United States with deadly force—such as trying to take Baldero at gunpoint—he would have no choice but to terminate them. But it would not be the act of justice that was taking down these Iranian killers and the members of the LDLS. It was simply a necessary act of self-defense, both on the individual and national levels.

Bolan, again checking in every direction to make sure no one was creeping up on his position while he was occupied with Uhlan, bent more closely over the man. "Uhlan," he said. "Dominique Uhlan. Can you hear me?"

Uhlan's eyelids, which had been drooping, began to flutter in recognition of his name. He managed to fix Bolan with a glassy stare. "I...yes," he said in accented English.

"Why are you here?" Bolan asked. He grabbed Uhlan, taking two handfuls of the man's commando sweater, and pulled him into a sitting position. "Who are you working for?"

Uhlan shook his head weakly. He would not answer.

"How are you tracking Baldero?" He jerked his chin at the damaged tracking device on the catwalk. "What does this device follow?"

Uhlan shook his head again. It was the last thing he ever did. His head reached the left side of his body and then lolled, suddenly nerveless. Bolan felt the man go completely slack in his grip.

Death had claimed him. He was forever beyond the soldier's reach, where so many of the Executioner's enemies eventually went—the only escape there was to be had from Bolan.

He stood. The were no sounds in the warehouse except his own breathing and the crackle of dying flames. He leaned over the railing of the catwalk and called to Baldero. The young cryptographer shouted back, but he was smart enough not to stick his head out. Bolan nodded at that, satisfied. He surveyed the killing grounds from his vantage high above.

They had planted a boot deep in the guts of the enemy forces, dealt them a blow they would not soon forget. He pressed the speed-dial button for the Farm. There was a lot to clean up, and a lot of work left to do.

He was only getting started.

The sunny afternoon was turning to amber and violet evening as the sun set outside the Washington, D.C., offices of James Tatro. Officially, Tatro was only a middle-ranking operative within the Department of Homeland Security. Unofficially, Tatro and those who answered to him knew that a great deal of one's authority was determined by how much you *took.* The rest was what others assumed.

That philosophy had served him well at DHS. He'd started small, then worked his way up, finding ways in which he could exploit the system for gain. Whether it was issuing false travel visas or simply looking the other way—and arranging for others to look the other way—when it came to the activities of certain powerful and well-funded entities who wanted access to the United States, well, what did he care? The other intelligence agencies, military arms, law enforcement divisions, and countless other parties had to have something to justify their budgets, didn't they? It wasn't as if Tatro was punching travel documents for the 9/11 hijackers, or something. He was just making a side income doing things that, in the grand scheme of things, really didn't matter—or so Tatro reasoned.

That had been the case until recently, at least.

Tatro had a hobby, and that hobby was cryptography, computers, software coding…anything complex like that. He didn't truly understand all the intricacies of it, of course, but it made him feel smart and interesting to immerse himself in geek codes and weighty intellectual doings. Once it had even gotten him laid, when he told the woman he'd picked up at a bar that he spent his spare time finding new ways to decrypt coded enemy transmissions. It sounded like something out of a movie because he'd made it up, but she hadn't known that.

The fact was that Tatro had gotten into government work because he'd wanted power, and when he saw that there was very little money in power as such, he'd had to find other ways to fund the very expensive lifestyle he was coming to enjoy. Expensive cars, a little coke, nice-looking women he picked up at the most expensive clubs in the D.C. area. Tatro knew how to live. He didn't intend to take any steps backward. That meant simply that he had to avail himself of what he could, where his position was concerned.

He'd always known that there was more money to be made in bending the rules than keeping them strictly. All he had to do was get more comfortable with seeking out clients and cutting deals. The internet had helped him do that. The very chatter his agency and others monitored for security threats helped him to find and contact, always anonymously, the individuals who needed what he could provide. That was how he'd shopped Baldero's program, once he'd convinced the kid that it was in his best interests to use the anonymous Tatro as a broker. Everybody would benefit, he'd told him.

What he hadn't counted on was the unexpected bonus. He'd shopped Baldero's encryption program, all right, selling it to those rogue nations who had the most bank to spend on something like that. He wasn't worried; he figured they could always get Baldero to knock out the decryption program if the encrypted communications from monitored nations started to become a problem. But then his customers had come back to him, separately, each one no doubt thinking they'd reinvented the wheel and come up with the idea on their own—they wanted Baldero, and they were willing to pay Tatro to help them get the man.

He hadn't wanted to do it, but the money they were throwing around, especially the North Koreans, was more than he could turn down. At their insistence he had been forced to reveal his identity. He might have been able to sell the French and possibly the Iranians on the idea without coming forward, but the North Koreans demanded that they know with whom they were dealing, partly because they wanted to make sure it wasn't a sting of some kind. Tatro suspected that they just enjoyed being domineering, too.

Well, he'd done it. He'd seen phenomenal sums transferred to his secret bank account in Switzerland. The North Koreans were promising even more if he helped them to scoop their competitors, and in the spirit of free enterprise, he was happy to do so. He'd crossed the line, here. He knew it. He'd gone from taking advantage of and even exploiting his position to what could only be seen as working against the interests of his nation, all for money.

Tatro did not, in fact, consider himself a traitor. It was just that the system was rigged. It wasn't fair. It was designed to reward only those who abused it. The more they abused it, the more handsomely they were rewarded. Why should everybody else in an already corrupt Washington see the gains of using their power to their advantage, but not Tatro? He could justify it in his mind that way, and that was enough. Yes, the North Koreans would end up with an unbreakable code and possibly the cryptographer himself, if they captured him alive. Yes, even if Baldero died, all the nations or splinter groups to whom Tatro had sold the program would have an unbreakable code that would cause problems for years to come. But, really, how big were those problems? It saved everybody some work if they didn't bother trying to decode the thing. The alternative was the endless race of breaking and creating new codes in an endless succession. It's not as if he'd sold enemy nations a weapon of mass destruction—or so that's what Tatro told himself.

As far as the DHS man was concerned, the only real problem was that his unexpected bonus had come with an unexpected headache. The Koreans, and especially this mission leader, Kim, who kept phoning to browbeat him, were becoming increasingly intractable and hostile. They treated him like a hired boy, and he supposed to some degree he had that coming. But the fact was that they needed to keep this operation under wraps if they were to get in and out, with Baldero or Baldero's scalp.

Instead, there was an all-out freaking war taking place in Virginia. He was not without his resources, and he kept a couple of Customs, Border Patrol and DHS agents on retainer to look out for his interests. They had helped him track all of the teams once they entered the United States, originally, and they had seen to it that the diplomatic credentials with which Tatro had provided the groups were honored. The teams and their weapons had gotten through. Tatro had done his best, through his hirelings, to keep tabs on them subsequently, reporting the movements of the others to the North Koreans.

They acted like he was trying to scam them or wasn't doing his job, and that pissed him off. It was Tatro, after all, who had provided the teams with the tracking units that keyed to Baldero's ultra-secure smartphone. That had been no mean feat, breaching the security of the DHS wiretap program in order to procure the trackers and establish the trace. Given that Baldero hadn't yet ditched his phone despite the fact that he was obviously being hunted, Tatro had to admit that this much had worked exactly as planned. Even if the man opened his phone and scanned it for bugs, he would find nothing. The little water damage sticker that was, in fact, not a water damage sticker at all, but a passive, low-frequency identifier that could be actively scanned by the DHS follower units, looked perfectly innocent. It would pass inspection even by a trained technician.

Once Tatro had used the resources of the government to trace Baldero's IP address—past several software and hardware firewalls—he had been able to lay the man's entire life before him on the screen. Credit history, wireless phone records, Internet Service Provider account data… He even had Baldero's high school and college transcripts. There was nothing the man could hide, and when Tatro had seen Baldero had paid extra for a next-generation secure smartphone only just recently being made available to current and former government employees, he had known that the newly initiated DHS tracking program would give him just the leverage he needed.

It had worked. The Iranians, the French and the North Koreans had all trusted him. They had been willing to pay him well for his help and his virtual guarantee that they would be able to find Baldero. Tatro had figured that once they were in the country, that would be that. After all, how long could one guy hold out against what was practically an enemy army on American soil?

Baldero, it seemed, was having the last laugh. He'd managed to escape repeated attempts by those idiots the Iranians to shoot him dead, and the French hadn't done much better. Even before those disasters, Tatro had gotten word that a bunch of ex-Mossad, operating more or less with the tacit approval of the Israeli government, were monkeying around. *That* worried him, because if the Israelis started snooping, they might get deep enough to uncover some link to Tatro that he hadn't been able to cover. God help him if they managed to capture one of the North Koreans and interrogated the prisoner. From what he'd heard, a motivated Israeli was nobody you wanted asking you questions while you were tied to a chair. As it was, he'd only found out about the Israelis through blind luck, and if he hadn't been able to pass on word to the North Koreans that they were operating here, they'd have assumed he had sold them out.

He was having a hard time covering up all of this in various ways at DHS. His reach to other law-enforcement and border agencies was long, but not infinite, and there was going to come a point at which his messing with the computer wouldn't put off the inquiries that might ultimately expose him. This, too, was troubling.

Then the Israelis and his departmental deceptions had quickly become the least of his problems. Reports were still coming in from the field about the single, presumably U.S. government operative who had interjected himself in the situation. Baldero's prospects of survival had risen considerably, and the bodies of foreign operatives had started piling up in almost comical numbers.

According to what he could ferret out, the man had identified himself as a Matt Cooper, claiming to be attached to the Justice Department. Tatro had made what he hoped were discreet inquiries, but he'd hit a brick wall as soon as he started asking questions about Justice's involvement in the "terrorist shootings" in Virginia. He'd decided to leave well enough alone. If they came back at him, and he hoped they didn't, he would try to play the whole thing off as just a jurisdictional dispute.

Tatro sighed. He began moving damaging files over to the most secure area of his computer, which could be accessed only by him. He had kept complete records of everything he'd done for this operation, primarily so that he would miss nothing when he had to cover them up or provide plausible explanations for them. He certainly didn't want to provoke an investigation, however, and if that did happen he didn't want his files where anybody could see them. He finished moving the last of the incriminating records and locked everything away. Entering the wrong code, or trying to break past his security protocols, would prompt his machine to completely wipe everything.

One of the reasons he didn't simply delete the files was that nothing was ever truly deleted from a computer. He knew that if he tried to delete them now, the only way to make sure they weren't accessed was to physically destroy the computer's hard drive. But, his files were safe for the moment, where no one could access them through the network without his numerous passwords. If, by some bizarre chance somebody tried, he'd get wind of it when his computer started to eat itself, and then he'd finish the job by reformatting the hard drive manually and dropping the computer on the floor. Maybe he'd shoot the thing for good measure, too.

The reminder that he had a gun in his desk comforted him somewhat. He didn't usually bother to carry it unless he wanted a date to "accidentally" notice it before he fed her a line about the dangerous work he was doing to protect the homeland. Somehow the idea that he had the means to defend himself, to shoot his way out, comforted him, even if it was somewhat unrealistic. If they caught him, he would be prosecuted as a traitor, and, given the extent of the mess the North Koreans and their competitors had managed to create, there wouldn't be any way to escape the blame for the conflagration. That being the situation, Jim Tatro was not about to be caught.

He opened the desk drawer and ran a finger along the black steel and plastic of the pistol. It was a Walther P-99, the same weapon James Bond carried in some of the more recent movies. It made him feel slick and polished, made him feel really important to handle that gun. At least it had before. He was starting to feel afraid, and the gun's presence was both a comfort and a grim reminder that things just might get serious.

He hadn't realized just *how* serious until his secretary buzzed him.

"Mr. Tatro," she said over the intercom, "there are a couple of visitors here to see you."

"Who are they?" Tatro asked suspiciously.

"They didn't say, sir."

"Well, ask them."

There was a pause. The secretary came back on the intercom. "They, uh, won't say, sir. They said you would want to see them. They said you had a mutual friend, a young lady named Virginia."

Tatro just about had a coronary right then and there. He couldn't stab the intercom button fast enough. He told the woman to send them in and then take an early lunch. She agreed to do so, and then the door to his office was opening and the North Koreans were there.

"Mr. Tatro," the smaller one said. He looked much calmer than his large, well-muscled, wild-eyed partner. "My name is Yoon Jin-Sang. This is my superior, Kim Dae-Jung." He pointed to indicate the crazy-eyed Korean. Tatro thought the man had hesitated before the word "superior," but it might have been his imagination.

"Are you nuts?" Tatro demanded, standing up behind his desk. "What are you doing here? Do you have any idea the risk you're taking, showing up at my office? You could expose the entire..."

"The entire what, Mr. Tatro?" Yoon said. "Do you hesitate to name precisely that with which you are involved?"

"Look, Yoom," Tatro said.

"Yoon," Yoon corrected.

"Yoon," Tatro said, flushing. "What are you people even doing in D.C.? Baldero's not here yet. There's nothing you can do here. Why would you risk exposure for all of us?"

"Mr. Tatro," Yoon said, "I believe my superior has already told you we are not happy about the involvement of this American agent."

Tatro again thought he heard something in the North

Korean's voice. Fear? Anxiety? It was hard to say, but the idea of this lone operative scared the man silly, if Tatro was anyone to guess.

Kim just glared. Tatro tried not to look at him.

"I've done what I can to determine who he is," Tatro said. "All I've managed to learn is that he's apparently with the Justice Department."

"Your Justice Department fields armed commandos?" Kim said, speaking for the first time.

"It might," Tatro said. "There are some black ops programs running through the aegis of Justice and a few other departments. It goes with the territory."

"Yet you can tell us nothing," Yoon said. It was not a question.

"I tried," Tatro said, hating the wheedling tone of his own voice. "I really did. They shut me down. Each time I tried to find out what Justice was doing on this a steel fire door shut in my face. Your best bet is to get Baldero before they can bring him back here."

"What do you mean?" Yoon asked. "Why would he be brought here?"

"Justice maintains a computer operations center in D.C.," Tatro said. "Several agencies use it. It's the sort of place where federal investigators have confiscated computers analyzed. They also do reconstruction work on damaged computers recovered from accidents, that sort of thing, and they have an entire department devoted to cryptography and code-breaking. Even if this guy, whoever he is, wasn't with the Justice Department, if he's with any federal agency at all, it seems pretty likely Baldero will end up there." He scribbled an address on a pad of paper and tore off a sheet, handing it to Kim. "This is the address. If all else fails, you have that."

"We could simply wait there for him to arrive and then snatch him."

"What?" Tatro paled. "No. No! You can't do that. For one thing, they have heavily armed security there."

"We can handle their security."

"Not like this!" Tatro protested. "You'll bring down the military on us, if you try to do it here in Washington. You're much better off trying to capture this Baldero before he gets here. Why would you have left him in the field? I thought you were following the other groups?"

"We were," Yoon said. "We still are. Do you think we are not capable of delegating a simple thing like surveillance to our senior people? It is what enabled us to make the trip to see you personally, Mr. Tatro. After watching your Justice man destroy a very large building and every armed man inside it, we thought perhaps there was much you were not telling us."

"You could have called," Tatro said. "You didn't have to risk blowing the whole thing!" He paused to wipe sweat from his forehead with a handkerchief he took from his pocket, sitting down at his desk. "I told you, I don't know anything."

"Yet you know enough," Yoon said in his articulate if accented English. "You know enough to embarrass my government when and if you are caught by your own. The presence of this very dangerous American agent tells us perhaps your people are not the simpletons you led us to believe them to be. You, Mr. Tatro, are therefore a loose end, and one we cannot afford to leave unaddressed."

Tatro saw it, then, in the eyes of the bigger Korean. An almost imperceptible nod passed between the two men. Yoon's was reluctant—Kim's was almost joyous. Then the big man was coming at him, reaching for him over the desk.

Tatro got his hand into the desk drawer and wrapped his fingers around the stippled plastic butt of the Walther. Kim reached out with one large hand and slammed the drawer shut on his wrist. Something cracked and Tatro screamed. He had a moment to regret sending his secretary away. There would be no one to hear his cries. There would be no one to call for help.

Kim grabbed Tatro's head over each ear and began to squeeze. Caught awkwardly in the desk drawer by his broken wrist, Tatro could do nothing but struggle feebly. Kim began slamming Tatro's head against the desk, again and again, leaving a dark red Rorschach blot on the cream-yellow paper of the blotter.

Tatro's vision went red. Through the haze of pain and approaching death, he looked up at Kim's twisted face, which was flecked with Tatro's own blood. Kim's eyes were bright with madness and arousal. Through the pain, through the sudden realization that this was it, this was his end, Tatro had a sudden, sickening realization.

He's enjoying this, Tatro thought. He's really enjoying this. It's fun for him.

His last thought, as death took him, was that the money hadn't been worth this. It hadn't been enough.

Not nearly enough.

13

Gambling that they'd have some time while the enemy regrouped after the devastating battle at the warehouse, Bolan had gathered up what remained of his munitions, made sure Baldero had survived the battle unhurt and commandeered an unmarked police car from among the responding officers on site. He'd again given his Justice credentials a heavy workout. The cops hadn't liked it one bit, but a call from a no-doubt overworked sleep-deprived Hal Brognola had squared it with them. The car was an older model, a Chevy Caprice with a lot of miles on its odometer, but it had a powerful engine and it responded readily enough.

Bolan had decided to hedge their bets by charting a roundabout route back through Charlottesville and then up through Harrisonburg, which would eventually get them to Washington. He had no reason to believe they weren't still being tailed, but the misdirection might confuse the enemy and could conceivably obscure their final destination. He didn't have much faith in that working, but it was worth a try. In combat, sometimes when you bluffed with a weak hand you were rewarded by an opponent's gullibility.

As they drove, Baldero was again tapping away on the

keyboard of his little smartphone, doing whatever it was he did when he wasn't running for his life. Bolan eyed him suspiciously.

"What?" Baldero asked.

"Are you sure there's no way they're tracking you through that phone?"

"Look, man," Baldero said, "I know that it's Secret Agent 101 to suspect a trace through the cell, or however you say it, but I've been over and over this thing. It's so secure it makes a bank vault look like a corner liquor store. I took it apart and swept it before I left. I checked all my clothes. I don't know how they're doing it unless ninjas snuck into my house and shoved a transmitter up my ass, okay?"

"We should destroy it to be on the safe side."

"I told you," Baldero said. "There's a lot of data stored on this phone. Encrypted data I can't just dump on a twenty-dollar USB memory stick from the nearest drugstore. I don't really want to have to reinvent the wheel when we get there, you know? I thought you wanted this decryption program written as quickly as possible."

"And I thought you said it would take a while," Bolan shot back. "I should have insisted before. We need to eliminate variables."

"Look, we're both a little wired," Baldero said. "Let's just, you know, let this go until we're both thinking a little more clearly."

Bolan glared at him. He weighed the pros and cons of simply taking Baldero's phone and smashing it, but decided he would have to live with its presence for the moment. If the man was so certain he needed the protected information on the phone, it was probably a good idea to preserve that data if they could. More and more, however, he was convinced that they were simply overlooking the most obvious means of tracking Baldero across the state.

They had reached Harrisonburg when they encountered

some extremely heavy traffic. They were forced almost to a standstill as the line of cars crawled along. The orange barrels of the construction zone they were entering seemed to stretch into infinity. Work crews were moving here and there, while many more construction personnel in orange vests were simply standing and surveying the work being done.

"Welcome to Virginia," Baldero said at last, looking up from his phone. Bolan caught a glimpse of the small screen. The cryptographer had been playing an electronic solitaire game.

Bolan glanced into the rearview mirror and could see nothing but the truck immediately behind him. Then he checked the side mirror.

His eyes narrowed.

The big yellow construction vehicle, some sort of loader with a large scoop on the front, was coming up fast on the driver's side. It was moving at what appeared to be its top speed. Bolan snapped his head around and then pointed out Baldero's window.

"Check your mirror!" he said.

Baldero leaned. "I see it!" he said. "Some kind of mobile backhoe-looking thing, coming up fast on this side!"

The cryptographer reached back and grabbed the pump shotgun he had retrieved, miraculously undamaged, from the ruins of the half-burned Crown Victoria. He had the Glock, too, which Bolan had allowed him to keep, figuring he couldn't abide having Baldero helpless when the man could at least try to defend himself. He was also no stranger to basic small arms, having checked out on pistols and rifles, however perfunctorily, while with the Air Force.

Bolan braced himself against the steering wheel. The large yellow machine smashed into the doors on his side, crushing the sheet metal underneath, producing a scream of metal on metal. The windows on both sides of the vehicle shattered, spraying the two men with pebbles of safety glass. On the passenger side, the second vehicle did the same. Drivers ahead of and behind them started honking. The one immediately behind Bolan pulled out and began driving across the median to escape, which gave the Executioner room to move. He jammed the column-mounted shifter into Reverse and slammed on the gas.

The engine roared and the rear wheels spun, burning rubber. The old Chevy began to tremble, rocking slightly back and forth, but it was stuck fast. The two heavy construction vehicles, far outweighing the beleaguered Chevy, had rammed into it on either side and held it fast. It was wedged between them so tightly that there was no way to open either door.

Bolan yanked the shifter again, trying for forward gear, then the lowest of the gears. He put the pedal to the floor, but succeeded only in creating a cloud of blue-white smoke as he burned rubber from the rear tires at an even faster rate.

"Baldero, we've got to—" he started to say.

"Do not move!" Ayalah Rosen appeared at the rear of the Chevy. Traffic began to move in front of the car, while other drivers, either oblivious to the drama unfolding before them or wishing very dearly not to be part of it, started to drive around the construction vehicles on the farthest point of either shoulder. Noam, holding an Uzi, covered Bolan from the front of the car. Two more Israeli operatives with shotguns flanked him, and a third with a similar pump-action 12-gauge moved to stand at the back with Rosen.

Noam cocked the Uzi.

"Down!" Bolan ordered. He grabbed Baldero and pulled him under the level of the dash, bending in his seat awkwardly to protect Baldero from above with his own body. The burst of automatic fire blew out the windshield and threw yet another layer of safety glass across the two men.

From the rear, the shotgun-wielding Israeli slammed the butt of his weapon into the rear window. It took him several tries, but he finally managed to break it out.

"Do not resist!" Noam shouted. "We wish him alive, but if you fire on us we will kill him!"

"He's got a point," Baldero managed to crack.

Bolan had the 93-R in his fist. "They blew out the windows for a reason."

"They're coming in, or they're going to try and drag us out?" Baldero said.

"Or they're going to—"

Bolan never got to finish his sentence, because by that time, the Israelis were already doing it. A series of hockey-puck shaped objects flew into the open windshield. Bolan managed to scoop up a pair that had fallen in their laps, tossing them back the way they'd come, but there were several in the backseat he couldn't reach.

"Eyes shut! Cover your ears! Mouth open!" he had time to yell.

The flash-bang grenades in the backseat went off, drowning them both in a fog of light and sound, hammering their senses with overwhelming percussive brutality. Bolan felt his head strike the steering wheel and tasted blood.

The next few minutes were like a dream. Bludgeoned nearly unconscious by the nonlethal sound-and-light grenades, Bolan could not move and could barely think as the Israelis swarmed over the vehicle. He was dimly aware of Rosen nearby, her perfume filling his nostrils and her black hair cascading down his cheek as she and another of the Israelis, possibly Noam, dragged him through the broken windshield and deposited him on the ground next to the construction equipment. Lying on his back on the shoulder, staring up at the large yellow-orange construction machine that had caved in his driver's door, Bolan's mind began processing disconnected pieces of information.

The Israelis had obviously stolen the machinery from the nearby construction site, either brazenly walking up and taking it, or threatening the workers with their weapons. Baldero was nowhere to be seen.

Some part of him understood that Baldero was being taken from him. He thought he heard shots, but he couldn't place them. There were sounds of struggling. Rosen said something, angrily, in Hebrew.

Bolan heard a car door slam shut, then an engine catch and start. He could hear the sound of tires rolling on grass, then asphalt.

The Executioner could not allow this. He was entrusted by the Farm and Brognola with a mission of utmost importance to the security of the United States. What was more, Baldero was an American citizen. They were not friends, no, but Bolan had to admit that he found the young cryptographer to be likable. He was damned if he was going to let foreign agents take the man away, to be tortured or killed in order to serve notions of national security held by some terrorist entity or splinter group.

He willed himself to focus through the pain and disorientation. Feeling as if he were floating above the pavement rather than lying on it, he managed to push off, rolling himself over. His face struck the ground, lightly, and his teeth clacked together. He could taste blood that was trickling from his nostrils and into the back of his throat, but he ignored that.

Bolan managed to pat himself down. His weapons were missing—all except the rosewood handled dagger in its sheath in his waistband, which had been either missed or ignored. Dragging leaden arms, he put his palms flat on the pavement, then pushed with all his might.

He managed to lever himself up and get his knees under him. Then, his head pounding so hard he thought it might explode, the Executioner wrenched his upper body up and back. He was kneeling, his vision blurred, floating purple and green blotches largely obscuring what he could see.

"He is up!" one of the Israelis shouted. He heard men approaching.

Bolan pushed himself to his feet in time to fall forward. As he did so, he toppled into the approaching Israeli, who said something in Hebrew—it might have been a curse—as the big soldier dragged him back down to the pavement. The Israeli was holding a pump-action shotgun. Bolan slammed a hammer fist on top of his opponent's face, crushing his nose. He managed to wrap his fingers around the shotgun and wrest it away.

Using the stock of the weapon like a crutch, heedless of the danger of blowing his own head off, Bolan pushed himself onto his feet again. Staggering like a drunk, he reversed the weapon. Three, no six, no three men were charging him, running in unison. Bolan realized he was seeing blurred images of a single man, so he targeted on the center figure and pulled the shotgun's trigger.

The recoil was strangely light, the sound of the round oddly flat. The man he'd shot doubled over, the breath pushed from his lungs, and fell to his knees. Bolan stared at the shotgun in confusion, his overwhelmed senses struggling to compensate.

A beanbag round, Bolan realized. The Israelis were using nonlethal beanbag rounds, like those used for crowd control.

He could hear the familiar sirens of police cars approaching. He had spent so much of this mission only steps ahead of both the enemy and the local authorities. Some part of that annoyed him, even as he struggled to regain his composure. Already, his vision was clearing.

The Israelis had turned and were making for a vehicle, a dark-blue Jeep Wrangler. Bolan leveled the shotgun and fired. The beanbag round took one of the running men in the back of the legs, felling him like a tree.

As Bolan approached the fallen Israeli's position, he

buttstroked him with the heavy wooden stock of the shotgun. He was finally aware of himself enough to identify the weapon: a sturdy Winchester Defender.

Two others had reached the Jeep. Bolan aimed and fired. The beanbag round was stopped by the car door as the fleeing Israeli closed it. Bolan cursed. His war bag was not with him; it might still be in the Chevy, or the Israelis might have taken it when they dragged him out of the car.

He kept on. He would take them with just his knife, if necessary. Bolan knew he had to find out where Baldero was being taken, had to recover the man before they could murder him or spirit him out of the country.

The soldier reached the driver's door and ripped it open before the man behind the wheel of the Jeep could pull away. The engine was running and the vehicle was in gear when Bolan yanked the man out and threw him to the pavement. The Wrangler began to move away, slowly, as Bolan planted his combat boot in the face of the fallen man. The Israeli was still, perhaps knocked unconscious.

Bolan managed to catch up with the Jeep and struggle into the driver's compartment, losing the shotgun in the process. He was not quite himself; he was still shaking off the effects of the flash-bang grenades. As he scrambled into position behind the Jeep's steering wheel, he growled, "You're going to tell me where Baldero's been taken." He started to reach for his knife.

The Israeli's eyes widened and he leaped out of the moving Jeep. Bolan mashed the brakes and got out, still unsteady on his feet, but motivated by righteous anger. These were foreign agents on American soil, foiling the interests of American security, endangering American citizens. Bolan was a patriot, yes; he was also, by his own choosing, a protector of the innocent, and that included the civilians these renegade Israeli agents were endangering.

He closed on the man, his knife in hand. "Where is he?" he demanded. "Where are your people taking him?"

The sound of a pump shotgun being racked filled his ears.

Bolan started to turn. As he did so, he saw the Israeli he had kicked was already on his feet.

The soldier tried to dodge.

The beanbag round hit him off center in the chest. He fell backward, unable to breathe, and the back of his head struck the pavement.

The motel room was large, while the motel itself was a particularly seedy, run-down stop on a side road—the kind of place that stays in business despite the fact that it has very little business to speak of. Baldero reflected that it was probably the sort of place rented by the hour for sordid trysts.

What he wouldn't give to be involved in one of those, right about now. Or sitting here being audited for tax evasion. Or getting a root canal. Anything but staring down Ayalah Rosen and her people.

She had come across all sultry with Cooper, probably because she was warm for his form, but she'd been nothing but a total bitch to him. When he'd finally come around from whatever nuclear hell-blast antipersonnel weapon they'd used on him, he'd been sitting in the back of her Grand Cherokee, with a Glock in his ribs and her accusing finger pointed at his face.

She'd told him he was going to create the decryption program for them. She'd also told him that he was going to do it in such a way that only her people—he wasn't sure if she meant her group, or the Israeli government that they kind of, sort of worked for or with, if he understood what Cooper had said about it—would be able to decrypt the encoded transmissions that employed his program. He'd told her that was pretty damned impossible, and that clearly she didn't understand how these things worked. She'd slapped him, and then the guy with the Glock had punched him in the jaw a few times, and he'd gotten kind of fuzzy about everything again.

Damn, but his head hurt.

He tried to picture what the big government agent would do in this situation. Baldero was pinned to a hotel-room chair by the wrists and ankles with duct tape, which they had also used to shut his mouth so he couldn't yell for help. Then they'd left him alone. He'd been sitting here for hours. It was dark outside. He was wondering if he'd live to see the sun come up again, but then, that's what he was supposed to wonder.

He knew how this game was played. He was former CIA, after all, and while he wasn't a field agent, he'd had some relevant orientation courses. He'd also sought out some other stuff—stuff he wasn't supposed to have—on file-sharing servers on the Web. He just liked knowing things.

He figured if he shouted, there wouldn't be anybody but Rosen and her thugs to hear him. The motel had looked pretty deserted when they'd arrived, which was probably why they'd picked it. Hell, they'd probably paid off the desk clerk to get lost while they were doing their thing here. It would fit with what he'd seen of them so far. They didn't want civilians in the cross fire any more than Cooper did, and that was saying something, since Cooper was apparently kind of obsessed with that sort of thing. He really was kind of an overgrown Boy Scout—an overgrown Boy Scout who had killed dozens of men, single-handedly, while Baldero watched. That was a sobering thought.

So what *would* he do in his situation? Probably use his razor-sharp jaw to cut through the duct tape, Baldero thought. Then he scolded himself for mentally screwing around. This was no time for joking. The Israelis had left him alone to give him time to wonder if they were going to leave him, or worry about what was to become of him, or other, similar psy-ops kind of bull. Well, he knew they were doing it, and knowing what was going on went a long way toward making it ineffective.

The problem was that he was pretty sure he'd heard Rosen tell one of her boys, in English, to grab the battery and some jumper cables out of the Jeep. Obviously he was meant to overhear that. He was supposed to be sitting here, crapping in his pants at the thought of them hooking up his nut sack to the electricity.

Well, he was worried, all right. They might only be making threats, but when he didn't cooperate, they'd start thinking there was no reason not to use that nice, big, heavy battery, since they had carried it to the room.

Baldero saw no reason to subject himself to torture, especially the electrocute-your-balls type of torture, but damn it, he'd had just about enough of being used by people like this. He was no goddamned traitor. He had tried to sell his program, yes, and the means through which he'd tried to do that hadn't been strictly legal, but he'd tried to make sure only friendly nations got the benefit of it. He sure didn't want a bunch of terrorists or even rogue agents of a friendly government to use the code to hurt his country. He cared, damn it. He cared what happened to America. He cared about his country's well-being.

That was Cooper for you, in spades. He was like some sort of…super-patriot. Baldero had to admit that the man's unflappable, almost stoic perseverance, his willingness to face danger for his country and to keep Baldero alive, really made him admire the big guy.

He paused for a moment. He would never have let the Israelis take him. Could they have killed him? He hoped not. Rosen's team had clearly tried to keep them both alive, right down to the way they'd neutralized Cooper and captured the car.

The door connecting Baldero's motel room to the one adjacent to it was thrown open. Rosen came in, looking angry but, well, pretty hot, anyway. Baldero stopped short of whistling at her in her skintight outfit. Who dressed like that? Was that what all the rogue spies were wearing these days?

"What is it," Rosen said, "that you find so amusing, Mr. Baldero?"

"You wouldn't understand." Baldero shook his head.

"Well, you will perhaps have to make me understand," she said. Her voice was low and full of menace. She snapped her long, slender fingers. One of the other Israelis, whom she'd called "Noam" and whom Baldero was starting to think was like her second in command, or something, came hobbling in carrying the heavy battery from the Jeep. The thing was enormous. Noam had a set of jumper cables coiled over his arm.

"Let's not get hasty, babe," he said, trying to keep up his bravado. If he could manage it, he would try not to break. He owed that much to Cooper. Maybe the big guy was trying to find him, even at this moment. Maybe he just had to hold out long enough for Cooper to show up, walk into the room and shoot everybody in the head. As near as he could tell, that was about as close to a plan as the Justice agent ever bothered to formulate, the incredible destruction at that warehouse in Richmond notwithstanding.

"You are brave," Rosen said, stroking the side of Baldero's face and toying with his hair, "but you are not very smart." Her tone had changed; she was almost purring, now. "Do as I say, and you will not be harmed." She leaned in close, so close he could look down the unzippered neckline of her jumpsuit and smell her perfume. She played with the collar of his shirt for a while, breathing hotly into his ear. He was starting to think she was the kind of woman who got turned on by doing things in front of witnesses.

She reached into his pocket, which produced some interesting possibilities, and came out with his smartphone in her hand, as if she had done something worth celebrating. "No more need for this, I think," she said softly. Then, more loudly, she went on, "Cooperate, and you will eventually be released or, if you like, you can stay with us, in our country, and work for my people."

"Let's talk about that," Baldero said. "What's the benefits package like?"

Rosen frowned. She drew back and slapped him again. "You will not be so flippant with the cables clamped to your—"

"Ayalah!" Noam called. He was looking out the window with his Uzi pointed at the ceiling of the motel room, holding the ratty curtains aside with one hand. Outside, Baldero could hear large vehicles stopping quickly. Gravel sprayed and brakes squealed.

"It is too soon!" Rosen said, an edge of fear in her voice. "They were not supposed to be able to follow us so quickly! They are not scheduled to be here for hours more!"

"It isn't them!" Noam said, watching. "Not the Iranians, and not the French, either. These men…men and a woman," he corrected, "they are Asian."

"So the initial reports were not simply witness conjecture," Rosen said quietly.

"You're kinda screwed, aren't you?" Baldero said. He braced himself for a blow, but she ignored him. Instead, she picked up her Glock from where it sat on the room's small table, checking its magazine and chambering a round.

The beautiful Israeli woman ripped open the connecting door and shouted in Hebrew to the men beyond. There was a lot of bustling around in there, and the sound of weapons being loaded and cocked. Baldero suddenly felt very, very exposed, taped into a sitting position in the middle of his motel room.

There was a very polite knock on the door.

Noam went to the door, hiding behind it with his Uzi held low, where he could bring it up and fire through the barrier.

"Yes?" Rosen said. She had forced her voice not to crack; the effort this took was obvious to Baldero.

"Give us the American," a voice said in accented English.

Noam brought up the Uzi, his last thoughts possibly of shooting through the door. But the enemy on the other side was faster.

Automatic weapons fire burst through the heavy outer door. Noam was cut down. With his last breath, his right hand clenched on the grip of the Uzi, spraying out its magazine in a long, wild burst that spiraled through the room. Rosen hit the floor, narrowly avoiding the stream of bullets. Baldero shrieked as they cut a path directly toward him, veering up at the last minute as Noam's fall pulled his arm and thus the barrel of the weapon up and back.

Baldero turned, his eyes wide, and saw the line of bullet holes carved by Noam's Uzi in the wall of the motel room. They tracked directly toward him at a level even with his head, then moved up and over him at the last possible instant.

Shrugging, the cryptographer threw himself, and the chair to which he was duct-taped, to the floor.

He watched in helpless horror as the few Israelis who were left fought valiantly, using their Glock pistols and Uzi submachine guns. One of them managed to bring a Galil from the adjoining room. He began firing out the window of Baldero's room, shooting at whatever vehicles were parked out there. Baldero could not see from his vantage point.

The door to the motel room was kicked open. The Israeli defenders concentrated their fire on the suddenly swinging door, which even Baldero could see was a mistake. As their attention was drawn, one of the attackers threw himself through the broken ground-floor window and came up with a large automatic weapon in his hands. The gun, which Baldero could not identify, had an integral sound suppressor. The Asian man who cradled the weapon in both hands let loose, cutting down the Israeli men still shooting. The man with the Galil took a round through the throat and several more through the chest. He dropped, trying but failing to scream.

Rosen punched a bullet through the attacker's head. She kept firing until her Glock locked open, and she was hurrying to reload when several Asian men swarmed into the room, automatic weapons in their hands.

The Israeli woman fought like a desperate animal. She kicked a chair into the path of the oncoming men, finishing her reload and blasting away with a fresh magazine in the well of her pistol. Several dead men lay at her feet when she ran empty again. This time, however, their numbers were too great—they simply rushed her. She started fighting them hand-to-hand, lashing out with brutal, effective kicks, doubling one over and punching another one so hard that Baldero thought he heard the man's jaw dislocate.

Then the Asian woman was there.

She was slim, a few inches shorter than Rosen, with delicate features that would have been beautiful on anyone else. The expression on her face was pure malice. She held a pistol of some kind in her hand, but as she moved to stand in the room amid the corpses of her comrades, she took the gun and tucked it into her belt. She smiled as she stared Rosen down. The Israeli woman was breathing hard and still held her locked-open Glock.

Baldero's smartphone was lying on the floor where Rosen had dropped it. The Asian woman looked down at it. She smiled and looked back to Rosen.

"You should have destroyed this," she said, "the moment you captured him."

"I imagine you are right," Rosen said, shaking her head. "We were perhaps too clever for our own good."

"And so," the Asian woman said, "you will die for your cleverness."

Rosen braced herself. She dropped the Glock and drew a folding knife from somewhere in her jumpsuit, snapping open the slim, daggerlike blade.

"Good," the Asian woman said. "Good." She jerked her right hand and suddenly there was a wickedly curved blade spinning in her hand, faster than Baldero could follow. She bent at the knees, her body taut, ready to spring. Baldero could see where this was going and he didn't like it, not at all.

As much as she had been willing to torture him to get what she wanted, there was no doubt in Baldero's mind that the Asian woman was the real villain here. His prospects were dropping with every minute he came closer to falling under the Asians' control.

He was really getting sick of this.

The women suddenly clashed in a flurry of blades, moving in and out at each other so quickly that Baldero could barely follow their actions. Blades sang through the air. The Asian woman moved easily, with a smile on her face, clearly enjoying herself. Baldero realized that she was toying with Rosen. At any time, she could have shot the Israeli woman, but she was enjoying the contest, playing around with her knife because she wanted to.

Rosen stabbed out, desperately, outmatched but unwilling to surrender. She managed to score a cut along the Asian woman's forearm, drawing a curse from her opponent. The Asian responded with a vicious slash that caught Rosen across the face, drawing a deep gash through the beautiful woman's cheek. The Israeli screamed and stumbled as the blade came back and cut across her torso.

The Asian woman moved in, grabbing Rosen by the arm and driving the Israeli woman's knife arm down and across her body. The curved blade in the Asian's hand drove deeply, and then Rosen's eyes were wide and her opponent seemed to be punching her in the stomach, again and again. Rosen's body jerked. She let out a hissing scream that was the most inhuman noise Baldero had ever heard. Then she stood there, seemingly supported by the Asian, staring into space.

With a laugh, the Asian dropped her opponent to the floor. She hit the carpet and stayed there, her hands going to her stomach as if to hold herself together. The Asian woman's hand and knife were covered with blood.

"Stupid bitch," the Asian said in English. She rattled off a series of commands in a language Baldero couldn't identify. He didn't know the difference between Japanese, Chinese and Korean, but her intent was clear enough. Several of her men picked up Baldero's chair. One of them produced a razor knife and slashed the duct tape holding the cryptographer down. Baldero was dragged roughly to his feet.

"I am Hu," the woman said to him. "You are my prisoner. You will cooperate or I will kill you."

Baldero had nothing to say to that. It seemed safer to keep quiet.

Hu went to the small bathroom and turned on the water. Baldero could not see her, but he knew what she was doing—she would be washing the fallen Israeli woman's blood from her hand.

After a few minutes, Hu reappeared. She folded the vicious, hawkbilled knife and made a final, spinning flourish with the weapon, then tucked it in her pocket, where a ring in the end of its handle projected for ready access. She eyed Baldero like a predator surveying its dinner. Then she barked a command to the men guarding him. They grabbed his shoulders and forced him up, dragging him roughly through the doorway.

He caught a last glimpse of Rosen, her eyes staring at the ceiling, her breath catching in her throat as the spreading pool of blood on the carpet beneath her grew ever wider.

It made him mad. Then he thought of something and started to laugh.

"What is it?" Hu snapped, looking at him. "What are you laughing about?"

"You people just made a really big mistake," Baldero told her.

"And what is that? What is it you find so amusing, American?"

"You really have no idea who you're messing with, lady," Baldero said, finding courage he didn't know he had, drawing strength from the idea that was beginning to form in his head.

"Spare me your pretensions," Hu said contemptuously, her accent doing weird things to the last word. "We know exactly who and what you are. You are nothing, Daniel Baldero, but a prize we have won in battle. You will be going nowhere we do not take you. Be grateful we do not simply kill you."

"Oh, hell, lady," Baldero said, shaking his head. He was seated uncomfortably between two stern Asian men, one of whom held a pistol on him. "It's not me you've got to worry about." He started laughing again.

"What is it?" Hu demanded angrily. "What?"

"I sure wouldn't want to be you," Baldero said, and he meant it. "I figure you've got hours, at most. Maybe less."

"Hours until what?" Hu grabbed the front of his shirt, leaning back from the front seat of the van in which she sat.

"It's just that I know a guy," Baldero said, "and boy, is he going to be pissed."

Bolan was angry.

It was a burning, righteous fury, and it fueled him as he held the accelerator of his borrowed state trooper's SUV. The big Chevy Tahoe, a silver-gray with blue lettering and an LED light bar, was carrying him swiftly toward Baldero's last known location.

He was no law-enforcement officer, but his Justice credentials and more phone calls from Brognola and Stony Man Farm had secured the reluctant cooperation of the Virginia State Police. He owed the state police a debt, in fact, for it had been their troopers who had found him, unconscious on the shoulder of the highway. He had been given medical attention, treated by the paramedics who responded to reports of a construction-related accident. Refusing a trip to the hospital, Bolan had allowed the first responders to verify only that he did not have a concussion. They had slapped a few adhesive bandages on him, and he had left them there, staring in amazement.

Procuring the truck had been easier than he might have thought, but he'd have stolen it if it had been necessary to do so. He had his foot to the floor and the SUV's lights and sirens going, cutting in and out of traffic that could not get out of his way fast enough.

In the first desperate moments after leaving the scene of Baldero's capture, he had placed a taciturn call to the Farm, informing Price briskly of what had happened.

"I don't know how," he had told her, "but you've got to find a way for me to pursue Baldero. There must be some way to breach whatever tracking system they're using. We've got to find him—he's lost if we don't."

"Striker," Price told him, "I think we've caught a break."

She explained to him that, since he had last contacted the Farm, a murder had been reported in Washington, D.C. That, by itself, was no surprise—Washington was, ironically, one of the more violent cities in the United States. This murder, however, was of a prominent figure in the Department of Homeland Security. James Tatro had been found dead in his office, the victim of a brutal beating.

"Tatro was making inquiries about the Justice Department," Price told Bolan on the phone, "attempting to determine, without anyone noticing that he was attempting to determine, just what Justice had to do with the terrorist attacks in Virginia. He kept asking about an agent Matt Cooper and requesting departmental cooperation regarding your particular involvement with the United States government."

"I'm listening," Bolan had said.

"It wasn't just a coincidence," Price said. "Given his activities just before his death and the brutal manner in which he was killed, in broad daylight in his own office, we suspected something connected to your mission. I had Bear and his team penetrate Homeland's network and poke around in Tatro's computer. Let me hand you over to Akira."

Akira Tokaido was an expert computer hacker, the youngest of the Farm's cyber team. When he came on the line, Bolan could hear the tinny backwash of the heavy metal music that played incessantly through the earbuds connected to the hacker's MP3 player.

"Striker, we found secure files," he reported to Bolan. "Tatro had a very sophisticated setup to safeguard his data, but we were able to circumvent that easily. He left complete records of his operation." Bolan listened, growing more amazed and more angry as Tokaido ran through Tatro's acquisition and sale of Baldero's program, as well as his dealings with rogue governments and his eventual selling out of Baldero to the North Koreans above the others. Finally, Tokaido had explained the secret DHS tracking program that had allowed the department—and Tatro specifically—to track Baldero's smartphone while also giving the foreign kill-or-capture teams this ability.

"We're transmitting to you now," Price said, coming back on the line, "the last known location data from Baldero's phone. It's a motel not far from your location."

"I'm on it," Bolan told her.

"There's something else, Striker," Price warned. "We've lost the signal, as of minutes ago. I don't know if we'll reacquire it."

"You won't," Bolan said, a flash of insight coming to him. "Barb, you've got to get in touch with the local authorities. Warn them off! If they try to respond to that signal they'll likely walk into another firestorm. Tell them all to stay away until they get the all-clear. I'd rather do this alone than have local cops or even Feds blunder into the kill zone."

"We could scramble military backup to you," Price offered.

"No time," Bolan said. "If my hunch is correct, this will be long over by the time they get there."

"What is it, Striker?"

"Whoever has captured Baldero did so knowing that phone was the key to finding him," Bolan said. "If they've destroyed it, it means they're confident they don't need it anymore. We're running out of time, Barb. Baldero's as good as dead or out of the country if I don't find him fast."

"Good hunting, Striker," Price had said. "And be careful."

"Striker out."

Thinking back to Price's last words as he pushed and bullied his way through the heavy Virginia traffic, Bolan knew that there was no way he would be careful. He was going to do what it took to get Baldero back, alive, and that was all there was to it.

He heard the sounds of gunfire as he closed on the motel. When the building came into view, he saw men with automatic weapons firing at one another from inside and outside the motel, some using the building for cover, others hiding behind vehicles in the parking lot. He caught a glimpse of one of the odd Iranian bullpup assault rifles, which meant at least one of the parties was the Iranian shooters. Could the Israelis be holed up in the motel with Baldero as prisoner? It was likely.

The men fighting in and outside the motel took notice of him and had no reason not to think he was a Virginia state trooper. They began firing in his direction. Bolan hit the brakes and then threw the SUV into Reverse, urging the Tahoe back the way it had come as bullets began to score the vehicles. One punched through the windshield, then a second. A third blew through the headrest of the passenger seat.

Bolan pulled the Tahoe through a tight curve and around a bend of the road leading to the motel. He had his personal weapons and what little was left in his war bag, recovered from the construction site where they had been found. He also had a couple of LAW rockets, leftovers he'd been carrying since the warehouse shootout.

It was time to bring the war back to the enemy.

He sat in the SUV and prepared his weapons. Then he reclined his seat back, pulled the 93-R machine pistol from its custom leather shoulder holster and flipped the selector switch to 3-round burst. Covering his eyes with one forearm, he blasted out his own bullet-starred windshield, spraying it with bursts until it was thoroughly perforated.

Replacing the pistol in its holster, he kicked out the remains of the windshield. Then he did something very dangerous—he pulled the pins on two LAW rockets and extended them, preparing them for firing. He placed the single-use weapons on the seat next to him, carefully.

He paused to swap the 20-round magazine in the 93-R for a fresh one, then he dropped the Tahoe into gear and stomped on the gas pedal.

He rode out the momentum as the big truck accelerated through the curve, its tires starting to squeal as he pushed it onward. The gunners, occupied with one another but still no less wary to external threats, began shooting at Bolan again as his vehicle drove into view. A bullet shattered the mirror on the driver's side. Several shots pocked the hood, raising sparks. Bolan pressed the accelerator to the floor and left it there, causing the big truck's engine to surge in its mounts and barrel him forward.

As he hurtled toward the motel, he raised one of the LAW rockets, armed it and pressed the trigger bar. The backblast filled the interior of the truck with fumes and blew out the rear window of the Tahoe. Bolan shoved his head out the open driver's window to clear the noxious cloud of gas.

The rocket flew ahead of him, struck the nearest parked vehicle—a van—and blew it apart, rattling windows in the front of the motel and showering the gunmen nearby with flaming debris. Bolan had just enough time to snap up the second LAW and trigger it before he had to slam on the brakes and turn the Tahoe's wheel hard.

The bone-jarring explosion of a second truck in the parking lot enveloped the Tahoe in a cloud of flame and shrapnel, some of it striking Bolan's truck as he managed to claw his way to a halt.

Bullets were striking all around him, but none was hitting very close. He kicked open the door of the Tahoe and drew both his pistols, the Beretta in his right hand, the .44 Magnum Desert Eagle filling his left. The Executioner strode forward, firing both weapons, picking his shots and making them count. As men began to fall around them, the gunmen panicked, their automatic fire becoming wider and wilder. Bolan moved among them, a vengeful wraith from which there was no escape. His bullets found their marks again and again. Where he passed, death followed.

There were shooters on the roof of the low building. They had to have climbed there from some unseen access point, perhaps simply jumping from the roofs of vehicles on the far side. Bolan was forced to drop back as slugs from their rifles found him, ricocheting all around him and spraying him with fragments of paving.

His guns boomed. He took one man under the chin and watched him roll down the slightly canted roof, landing in a heap on the pavement below. Another man, who was wielding a Colt SMG, sprayed an entire box magazine of 9 mm rounds across the shooter next to him, when Bolan's bullet caught him at an angle and caused him to fall, turning in place. The unlucky gunman who caught the blast was shredded at the pelvis and thighs, shrieking as he fell backward onto the roof and tried to hang on. One of the other gunners from below saw his precarious position and put a bullet through his brain, spraying him across the tarred roof.

"Do not shoot!" someone shouted. "Do not shoot! I surrender!" Bolan turned and saw a man throwing down his Colt rifle. *"Ne tirez pas! Je suis sans armes et aucune menace pour vous!"* Bolan held his fire in the heat of the moment, but one of the other gunmen did not. A ripping burst of automatic fire climbed up the man's body from crotch to neck, practically blowing him apart. He threw his arms out in supplication and cried out one last time before he fell to the ground in a wet, bloody heap.

Bolan fought his way toward the entrance to the motel room, leaving a trail of corpses to mark his path. Then he was kicking in the already bullet-riddled doorway. A man stood there, and when he saw Bolan, he dived to the floor. The room was a slaughterhouse, full of bodies, every conceivable surface covered in bullet holes and streaked with the blood of the fallen.

The triangular muzzle of Bolan's Desert Eagle followed the figure down—and stopped. The man surged to his feet with difficulty, dragging Ayalah Rosen with him. She stared at Bolan, her eyes glazed, blood soaking the front of her jump-suit. Her arms were wrapped around her abdomen in a death grip. Her knuckles were white, and her face was ghastly pale. Bolan knew what he was seeing. Rosen had lost a great deal of blood.

Bolan recognized the man from the files. He was Hassan Ayman, the senior Iranian. He had an arm wrapped around Rosen's throat, choking her as he held her up by the neck. Bolan could see she was only barely hanging on. Ayman had the barrel of his SIG-Sauer clone pressed against her head. He jerked his chin, gesturing toward Bolan and then to the floor. His meaning was clear. He wanted Bolan to drop his weapons.

Bolan lowered the barrel of the Desert Eagle. His hand tightened around the grip of the 93-R, which was held low against his leg.

"Put her down," he said.

"You," Ayman said, sneering. "You face Hassan Ayman!"

"Yeah," Bolan said. "I figured that."

"Put down your weapons! Down! Put them down!" Ayman yelled.

Bolan said nothing. Finally, surveying the dead men in the room, he said, “You’ve been busy.”

“As have you,” Ayman said grudgingly. “It was you, in the large building, was it not? With your mines and your explosives.”

“You were there?”

“I waited outside, guiding my men.” Ayman nodded. “I know what you did. What you are capable of doing.”

“A real lead-from-the-front kind of guy, are you?”

“Silence!” Ayman shrieked. “I will not be mocked, not by you! We are Iran! We will have our due!”

“From where I stand,” Bolan said, “your ‘due’ is a bullet.”

“Do you think you can scare me so easily?” Ayman demanded. “We have killed the French! They are all dead, all! I have seen to it this day. You deal only with me!”

“I don’t make deals with terrorists,” Bolan said.

Bolan’s left wrist cocked up from his waist and he fired a single round from the hip. The bullet bored through Ayman’s right eye. The Iranian terrorist folded at the knees, dead where he stood. Ayalah fell with him and Bolan rushed forward to catch her. He placed her on the blood-soaked carpet as gently as he could. He was very aware that they were surrounded by a small mountain of dead bodies. Nothing moved.

Rosen’s eyes were closed. Bolan feared she might be lost already. When he lifted her, slightly, her eyelids fluttered open.

“Cooper,” she said weakly.

“I’m here. Don’t move. I’ll call an ambulance.”

“No,” Rosen said, her voice a whisper. “It is too late. I am…I am passing to the other side. But there is no reason…to take your Baldero with me…” She faded for a moment. Bolan shook her gently to wake her.

“Baldero?” he asked. “You know where he is?”

“We…were very clever,” Rosen said, trying to rally. She

fixed Bolan with a desperate gaze, the light slowly fading from her eyes. "We were tracking Baldero through his phone."

"I know about that," Bolan said. "The signal has been lost."

"Destroyed." Rosen managed to shake her head. "But we had planned…to destroy it. We wished to draw…the French and Iranians…to us, so we let them continue to follow… We had thought to…blame them, escape with Baldero but leave them here, to be found by you, or your police… They would be the villains, and we would disappear."

"What happened?"

"The…North Koreans…" Rosen said. "We were…right. They found us. Too soon. We were not ready… They have taken your Mr. Baldero and they have killed me."

Bolan's eyes widened. Rosen was fading fast. Her eyes started to roll up into her head. "Ayalah!" He used her name, trying to bring her back. "Ayalah!"

It worked. She looked at him again, one last time. "I put…a tracking device of our own on Baldero. It is…under his collar. The frequency is…1575.42. You can trace him through that, it is L1 band… We did not wish to risk losing him…if you found him and took him back… But there is no one else… and you are all that remains."

"Thank you," Bolan said quietly.

"Who…who are you?" Rosen said. There was no sound in her voice anymore. She mouthed the words.

"Mack Bolan," he told her.

"I…I know this name…" Rosen breathed. It came out as a rattle. Then she was staring at nothing, and Bolan held a dead woman in his arms. The faintest trace of a smile touched her lips.

Bolan reached out and gently closed her eyes. Then he knelt and picked her up, carrying her bloody body from the charnel house and out into the parking lot. There was a small area of grass near the now-deserted motel office, and a large tree grew there. He took Rosen to that island of life in this otherwise still killing ground and placed her gently under the tree. Then he went to the bullet-riddled Tahoe, found a state trooper's jacket inside it and brought it to cover her.

She had not been his ally. But neither had she truly been his enemy, and she had died fighting the predators, the animals, who tore and clawed at the fabric of civilized society, who sacrificed innocent life without a second thought, who killed for gain and for their whims and at the behest of their criminal governments. He had been prepared to shoot her or her troops if that had been the difference between success and failure in his mission, and he was morally justified in doing so. But even as his foe, she had died closer to the side of right than she might have imagined in her most private of moments, and Bolan would count her as an almost-friend in his never-ending war. He had seen many good men and women struck down over the years. She was, most simply, yet another person to add to their ranks, yet another corpse to tally in an impersonal balance sheet of collateral damage. Yet she had been more than that. The Executioner would not permit himself to see her as a number, for down that road led the loss of his humanity, something he would never abide.

With his guns reloaded and again ready at his sides, he checked the death zone for survivors and found none. Then he called the Farm and told them what Rosen had revealed. Price promised to put Kurtzman and his team on the problem right away—they would call him the second they learned of Baldero's location and could provide Bolan with a means of following Rosen's signal. Whatever tracking device Rosen herself might have had was nowhere to be found. That much of her plan had died with her.

While he waited, Bolan took photographs of as many of the dead as he could, transmitting the photos to the Farm for analysis and identification. It wasn't long before they started to come back as SMS messages, cross-indexed to dossiers that were fed to him by the Farm's computers. The high-capacity memory card in his secure sat phone digested them all.

He glanced through the intel, impatient to get on the road once more, waiting for the Farm to give him a heading. He had faith in Kurtzman's skill and in the team of cybernetics professionals backing the wheelchair-bound computer genius, but that did not make the waiting any easier, knowing Baldero was in the hands of a North Korean kill-and-capture group.

The Executioner stepped into the motel room once more, intending to give it a final check.

A minute later, a tall, black-skinned man tried to cut his head off.

The dark-skinned man swung a heavy kukri at Bolan's neck, missing by inches when the soldier ducked and rolled. He threw a side kick into the black man's thigh, shocking the muscle there. The kukri-wielding newcomer shouted and fell to one knee.

Bolan threw a combat boot up under the man's chin and knocked him onto his back. The Executioner's hand found the butt of the 93-R machine pistol as he did so, and the compensated snout of the weapon bore inexorably on target. Having lost his kukri, the man went for a revolver tucked into his waistband. Bolan shot him through the head before he could complete the draw. He died in the middle of a pile of corpses, instantly becoming just one more body for the tally.

The soldier stepped outside, his gun up and ready. He heard someone shout, "Rafiki! You bastard!" Then he was taking throaty automatic fire from somewhere in the lot, as heavy slugs bore into the doorjamb, rending the already splintered wood to smaller pieces.

Bolan ducked back behind what little cover the flimsy motel doorway provided. He could tell the slugs were .45 caliber by the sound they made and the holes they left. He spotted his attacker, finally—a slight, fair-skinned man with dirty blond hair was crouched behind one of the scorched van hulks, laying down an impressive field of fire with an old M-3 A-1 Grease Gun. He wielded the WWII-era weapon as if he knew how to use it.

Bolan could not imagine whom these new parties were, unless they were stragglers left from the French contingent. They certainly were not Iranians or North Koreans. The soldier holstered his weapon and scooped up a fallen Khaybar rifle. He worked the bolt and was rewarded with an unfired cartridge that flew over his shoulder. The magazine was close to full. He snatched a couple of spares off the corpse whose rifle he had appropriated, dropping these into his shoulder bag. The war bag was very light; he was running low, and the Iranian weapon would help him stretch out his remaining ammunition.

Bolan waited while the gunner ran his weapon dry, then fought with the stick magazine and the ungainly cocking handle on the M-3 A-1. In this pause, he shouted, "I am an agent of the United States Justice Department! Throw down your weapon and the killing can stop!"

"Up yours!" the little man yelled back. He emptied another magazine into the wall next to Bolan, very nearly managing to punch his heavy rounds through the soldier himself. Bolan was forced to dive across the opening and take cover on the opposite side of the doorway.

There was a second pause—the gunner was fighting with his weapon again, trying to get it reloaded. Bolan dashed out from behind cover, rising from his knees to his booted feet, and charged. The man with the Grease Gun was just yanking the weapon's bolt when the Executioner found his angle, snapping the Khaybar to his shoulder and firing a single round. The light rifle bullet drilled a neat hole through the gunman's head. He died with a confused look of disbelief on his face. Then he fell forward into the gravel-strewed asphalt.

"Not bad," a voice drawled behind him.

Bolan risked a look over his shoulder, the Khaybar held out to his side. The short, stocky man behind him held a 1911-type pistol on him. He was dressed in camouflage fatigues and wore a black beret on his head, cocked rakishly to one side. The beard framing his wide, round face was neatly trimmed.

"Rafiki and Skarsgard were pretty good," the man drawled again, his voice pure West Virginia. "But they weren't near as good as me. Tell me, buddy, just who are you? Turn around and look at me, but don't get squirrelly with that gun."

Bolan did as the squat man ordered. "Isn't that my line?"

"Fair enough, fair enough," the bearded man stated. "My name is Roland Collier." He paused expectantly. When Bolan said nothing, he frowned. "Maybe you've heard of me?" he asked.

"I can't say I have."

"Well—" Collier looked annoyed "—I can't help it if you're not up on the competition."

"What competition is that, exactly?" Bolan asked.

"Well," Collier said, moving closer, standing before the Executioner with the gun held casually in his right hand, "I'm like you. I'm a soldier for hire. I assume that's what you are, lone-wolfing it as you've been doing across this fine state."

"If you're a mercenary, who do you work for?"

"Why, that's privileged information, pal," Collier scoffed. "I'm surprised you'd even ask. Now, you just set that rifle down."

Bolan put the weapon on the deck. A gleeful Collier took a step closer—the step the soldier had been waiting for, though he could scarcely believe his good luck.

"What is your involvement here?" Bolan asked. Collier was a talker, obviously. His need for Bolan to know who had beaten him was palpable. He might be willing to let something slip—the Executioner could use his vanity against him.

"I've been following this sorry bunch across the state," Collier admitted. "Figured to take your Dan Baldero right from under these Jews, here—" he nodded toward the motel "—but I guess our timing was off. When we got here, the towel-heads and the frogs were already busy whacking each other. Figured we'd stand off until they settled it. Then you came along."

"You were following them."

"Yeah," Collier said. "Course, we were following the North Koreans, and they started moving a lot faster than we figured. We had to stay far enough back so they wouldn't spot us, right? But they got away and by the time we got here figuring to maybe still find Baldero, well, that was all she wrote. You were busy punching their tickets."

"So you don't know where Daniel Baldero is," Bolan pressed.

"No, but that's not going to be so hard," Collier said. "Those North Koreans can't be too far. We'll pick them up and follow them, then take that good ol' boy right away from them. Hell, it hasn't been so hard tracking this entire sorry parade of fools up to now. We could have followed you by the smoke and the bodies alone."

"Touché." Bolan nodded.

"Now then," Collier said, "you just lower that rig you're wearing. Bag, too. And take the hogleg out from your belt and put that on the ground, as well."

Bolan did as he was instructed. "If you think you're going to question me, I'll warn you that you won't get anything," Bolan said. Normally he wasn't given to such you'll-never-get-away-with-this speeches, but it might get Collier talking again. He'd learned a lot already.

"I'm not going to torture you, buddy." Collier grinned. "I'm just gonna shoot you."

Bolan's hand whipped out, faster than a rattler, and slammed the inside of Collier's wrist, driving his gun hand out and away from Bolan's body. As he did so, he moved in and slammed the web of his hand against Collier's throat, knocking the man back. The merc lost his pistol and stumbled backward, choking and coughing.

Bolan started to bend and snatch up one of his guns, but Collier was tougher than he looked. He charged forward, throwing his arms around the Executioner, dragging him down in a bear hug. The stocky man squeezed for all he was worth. Bolan could feel deadly pressure against his ribs.

The Executioner brought his head forward, snapping his forehead into Collier's nose. The mercenary bleated and lost his grip. Bolan kicked him off and then regained his feet. Collier, backing away a few paces and wiping one meaty hand across his swollen nose, put up his hands, balled into fists.

"All right, then," he said. "All right. It's been a while since I had me a good street fight, boy."

Bolan realized, suddenly, what seemed so wrong about the encounter. He was used to dealing with deadly professionals, with the worst, most vicious international and domestic terrorists imaginable. This Collier, who had somehow managed to attach himself to the hunt for Baldero, was an amateur—an also-ran. He clearly had no idea what he was doing and, worse, he appeared to think he was every bit as "bad" as the words of his big mouth promised.

It was almost a refreshing change, the Executioner thought. It was almost a relief, to be dealing with someone of Collier's caliber.

Collier misinterpreted the look of surprise and recognition on Bolan's face.

"You scared, asshole?" he said, dancing around, his fists tight under his chin in a fighting stance. "You *should* be. This is Roland Damned Collier you're facing. I've been street fighting since I was a damned teenager, son. I'm going to chew you up and spit you out. I'm going to make you sorry you were ever born. I'm going to—"

Bolan slapped him in the face.

Collier stopped, a look of shocked amazement on his reddening features. Bolan stepped in again, a little half-step that put him in range, and backhanded Collier across the face again, bloodying the man's lip.

"Shut up," he said.

Collier screamed in rage. He stepped forward, swinging wildly. Bolan figured the man's heavy fists would do some damage if they connected, but Collier was badly off balance. Bolan blocked a wild hooking punch and then slammed a foot against the man's lead ankle. A bone snapped, and Collier folded on the damaged ankle, screaming.

Bolan let him fall. The squat man hit the paving hard, and something else broke as he did so—possibly an elbow. He was practically shrieking with the pain. The soldier backed off a few steps, retrieved his weapons and put them back on. He did not holster the Desert Eagle.

"Mr. Collier," he said, as he stood over the fallen mercenary, "you have just assaulted an identified representative of the United States Justice Department. You have also interfered in a government operation, threatening the interests of the government and of national security, by your own admission." Bolan did not normally arrest people, for as he had thought to himself many times during this mission, he was no law enforcement officer. He was a soldier, doing a soldier's job. Yet he could not bring himself to kill Roland Collier like this, as the pitiful fool lay crying out in pain on this motel parking lot. In a way, Collier's pitiable state was a welcome change from the brutal world in which the Executioner walked every day.

"Please!" Collier said. "I'll talk, I'll talk! Don't kill me! Don't kill me! Oh, God, I've seen what you do! Don't murder me, please! I'll turn State's witness! I'll tell you anything you want to know! It was Wassermann, Sirus Wasserman!

Sirux-Gibbmann, that's his company! He paid for it! I'm just an employee! I'm just an employee!"

Bolan shook his head. He turned to go for the Tahoe or what was left of it, knowing that its radio could connect him with the authorities. He would have them come for Collier and put him in protective custody. Then he would call it in to the Farm, and Price or Brognola could see to it that Collier was dropped down an appropriate hole after he had been debriefed. Bolan shook his head again, thinking that the killing grounds in which he stalked was no place for—

Some instinct, some change in the very atmosphere around him, made him turn. The tone of Collier's bawling had changed, as had the expression on his face. He was pulling a snubnose revolver from a holster on his good ankle. The weapon came up, looking like a child's toy in his thick fist, the hammer coming back…

Bolan dropped to one knee as he swiveled, snapping a single .44 Magnum round from the Desert Eagle. The 240-grain slug punched through the center of Collier's face and toppled him backward, splaying his brains across the pavement beneath him.

It had been a sobering reminder to the Executioner. Even fools could be dangerous.

As if on cue, his phone began to vibrate.

"Striker," he said quickly.

"We have position data, Striker," Price told him. "Baldero is being held in Alexandria. At least, the bug your Israelis planted on him is transmitting from there, not far from the port."

"It makes sense," Bolan said. "They could charter a boat, or meet one, and take it down the Potomac to Chesapeake Bay. Maybe even travel from there to the Atlantic, depending. A North Korean sub or freighter or something could be waiting for them. They'll transport Baldero out of the country and he'll be back in Pyongyang before you can blink."

"It looks that way, Striker," Price said. "We are transmitting the GPS coordinates to you now."

"Barb," Bolan said, even as he ran for the Tahoe, jumped in, and started the roughly idling engine, "I need another piece of information." He slammed the gearshift into Reverse, pulled out and dropped the truck into Drive, barreling down the motel's access road. "I need to know who or what a Sirus Wassermann is, and something called Sirux-Gibbmann. Also, see if you can get me anything on a Roland Collier."

"Who's Roland Collier?"

"Who *was* he," Bolan said. "I just shot him. I think he was a pretender to the game, but he gave up this Wassermann before he died."

"Striker, this is Bear," Kurtzman's voice cut in. "I can answer part of your question immediately. Sirux-Gibbmann is one of the world's biggest computer software companies, and Wassermann is the eccentric owner and CEO. He's legendary in the programming world. And he's got his fingers very, very deep in fields like cryptography."

"The plot thickens," Bolan said. "Does he have any history of hiring private soldiers?"

"More than," Kurtzman said. "Gibbmann left the country a while back, fleeing some inconvenient charges in the U.S. legal system. He's been living in part of what used to be Liberia ever since, paying off the Liberians and whatever government the Ivory Coast claims. He's rumored to have a private army of soldiers of fortune guarding his headquarters, both as a bulwark against the otherwise anarchic country he's adopted, and also because he's got any number of enemies. Even his friends are pretty shady, for that matter. You name it, from the Justice Department to Interpol to organized crime, there are plenty of people who either buy services from Wassermann or who would gladly see him dead."

"Well, however he got wind of it, it looks like this Wassermann was another contender for Baldero's program," Bolan said. “He had a team of mercenaries on-site. I’ve capped at least three of them, I’d guess, though it’s getting hard to tell who’s playing for what team without a scorecard down here. Collier might or might not have been in charge of them. You’ll want to have Hal poke around and maybe talk to Interpol. If Wassermann has the program and is willing to kill for it, he may be bucking for rogue state status all by himself.”

“We’re on it, Striker. You’re on your way?”

“Already doing ninety,” Bolan said. “Baldero’s coming to Washington before I’m through, and anybody who tries to stop me will pay. Striker out.”

17

The tracking data the Farm had fed him led Bolan to a safe-house that appeared to be a closed curio shop, in a quaint but heavily commercialized neighborhood in Alexandria. He had called ahead and had the Farm use local law enforcement to quietly clear out any civilians in the neighborhood. That, combined with what Bolan was about to do to this small portion of Alexandria, would probably give Brognola heartburn enough to last him a couple of weeks, but there was no alternative. The North Koreans were holding Baldero within that structure—if the cryptographer was still alive. There was no reason to drag the body about with them if the man was dead, after all. Bolan knew the chances were good that Baldero was inside awaiting rescue.

Rescue was coming—and hell with it.

He spotted a sentry peering out from blinds blocking a window that fronted the shop. The oddly profiled weapon in his hands appeared to be a Chinese Type 85. It was a capable submachine gun, firing 700 rounds a minute from a 60-round magazine, chambered in 7.62 mm. The weapon this sentry held appeared to be a suppressed version, which meant it would be loading Type 64 subsonic ammunition rather than the hotter, lighter Type 51.

Waking into a firestorm of either was not going to help Baldero.

Bolan, from his vantage in a line of cars parked on the street, hoped his shot-up Tahoe would not be too noticeable. He considered the problem. Any attempt to raid the building, with or without help—and he had refused assistance again when speaking to the Farm about clearing the neighborhood, knowing that more troops would only increase the risk to Baldero—would cause the North Koreans to either flee or, worse, kill Baldero to cut their losses before they escaped. That could not be permitted. A surgical strike was called for.

Bolan was the scalpel.

There was little point in debating the issue. The time for action was here. He made sure his weapons were secure in their holsters and that he carried a full complement of spare magazines, drawing from the last of the stores in his war bag. Then he screwed the custom-built suppressor to the threaded barrel of his Beretta 93-R, held the pistol low against his leg and walked up to the front door of the curio shop.

He rapped on the door.

"Go away!" a voice said from within. "Closed!"

"Candygram," Bolan said, deadpan.

"You go away!" came the response. "We closed! No business today!"

"I have business today," Bolan said.

Knowing that at any moment, a shotgun blast or a burst of 7.62 mm fire could chop him in two at the waist, Bolan took a step back and planted a combat-booted foot in the door next to the doorjamb. The wooden door splintered and slammed inward, reverberating off the wall inside.

The Executioner dived into the room.

Multiple voices screamed at once. The metallic sound of

bolts being pulled back filled the air. Bolan rolled and twisted on the floor. The suppressor tracked from man to man, and he started firing, triggering 3-round bursts.

The slapping of the subsonic hollowpoint rounds was like the clapping of hands in the small room. Bolan shot one man through the chest, dropping him. He shot another in the face. He shot a third across the knees, dropping him to where he could target him better, and then blasted him from the neck to the forehead. Twisting on his back, he braced the Beretta between his legs and targeted the closed, adjoining door, which led farther into the little shop.

The last of the bodies in the room hit the floor with a heavy thud.

A voice called out from the room beyond. Bolan recognized the language as Korean. Another voice answered the first, this one a woman's. Her tone was angry. The first voice was cut off in midsentence.

Bolan waited.

He could hear the doomsday clock ticking in his head, as he always did when he entered a free-fire zone like this one. There was much movement in the room beyond. Bolan cut his eyes left, then right, surveying the room quickly, always keeping the adjoining door at least in his peripheral vision.

A dead man's hand was curled around the familiar lines of a Tokarev TT-33 pistol, probably also chambered in 7.62 mm. The thought came to Bolan idly; random fragments like that often came to him as he fought, the fog of war occupying his gross motor functions and his reptilian hind-brain, while his higher functions went along for the ride, calling the shots like a general transmitting orders from behind a phalanx of troops.

"American?" the woman's voice finally called from within. Bolan saw no reason not to answer her. The alternative was a standoff from which there could be no escape, as each side was determined not to move first. Instead, he would force the issue. He knew where this was likely to go. He rolled out of the path of the door and set his Beretta 93-R on the floor. Then he reached out and plucked the Tokarev from the nearby dead man's fingers.

"I'm here," Bolan said. As he did so, he checked the magazine of the Tokarev, racked the slide and caught the ejected round in his palm. He reloaded the weapon and chambered the first cartridge. Then he cocked it and, very carefully, slipped the Tokarev into his shoulder holster, tugging it down so that the grip showed prominently. He picked up the Beretta and unscrewed its suppressor, tucked that into his back pocket and put the cocked gun, its safety off, into the back of his waistband. He drew the Desert Eagle and crabbed up into a crouch and then to his feet against the wall.

"Surrender or we kill him," the woman said simply.

"I think if you had orders to kill him, you'd have done so already," Bolan said.

"Don't do me any favors!" Baldero called. There was a soft thump from the other side of the door, and Baldero cursed. It sounded like he'd gotten the butt end of somebody's pistol for his outburst.

"We will open the door," the woman's voice said. "You will drop your weapon."

"I will lower my weapon," Bolan said. "Or we don't talk at all."

"Very well," the woman answered.

The door creaked open. Baldero was sitting in a chair in the storeroom of the shop, his hands bound with fabric tape. His feet were free, which was an important piece of information. He did not appear to be otherwise restrained. Two Koreans were standing behind him. The woman had a curved kerambit folding knife open and at Baldero's throat. She was standing directly behind him, caressing his head with her free hand, playing with his hair.

"If you try to shoot me," the woman said, "my men will

raise their weapons. You will die in the attempt." The two Koreans flanking her had Type 85 suppressed submachine guns. They held them at the ready but were not pointing them.

"If they try," Bolan returned, "I will shoot you in the head." He held the Desert Eagle low along his leg, in an imitation of the Korean gunners' stance. He gestured with the weapon, making sure she saw the motion, but he did it slowly, lest the gunners get nervous and open fire. She nodded slightly, her eyes alight with something like bloodlust that was very near arousal.

"What is your name?" she asked.

"Cooper," Bolan said. "Justice Department."

"I am Hu," the woman said.

"She's the one who did Ayalah, man," Baldero said. "She's a murdering bi—"

Baldero's outburst was cut short when Hu pulled his head back and placed the curved blade of the kerambit against his skin. Suddenly, the cryptographer was very quiet.

"He is right," Hu gloated. "I killed the woman the Jews sent. We have killed most of those sent against us, and we have taken the prize. As we always knew we would. But as a sign of..."

"So," Bolan said, "let's come to an agreement." He thumbed down the hammer of the Desert Eagle and made a show of placing the weapon in the front of his waistband, in easy reach.

"Yes," she said. "Yes, let us do that. You want him alive. We want him alive. But we will kill him and you will get nothing, if you try to stop us. You will give us safe passage out of here. We will be meeting a boat, which will take us to the bay and beyond."

"I thought so," Bolan said. He placed his left hand on his hip in a cynical gesture.

"Just so." Hu nodded. "You will make sure this vessel has

safe passage. You will not interfere with it. Your government will not interfere with it."

"And?" Bolan asked.

"I have a pair of associates who will be joining me. They will not come here if they see that the perimeter has been breached, but they will not be far away. You will not be able to catch them. They have been traveling covertly, aware that they could be picked up, playing a very cagey game with your fools of soldiers and police officers. You do not know that death stalks your highways, but it does."

Bolan made a gesture that looked like rotating a crank. "Any time you'd like to make your point," he said finally.

"Safe passage applies to my two comrades, regardless of whatever crimes you think may permit you to hold them," she said. "You will know them when you find them, if somehow you do."

"Us fools? I thought that was impossible." He was deliberately needling her, trying to keep her annoyed and off balance.

"You *will* give them safe passage," Hu said. "I had expected them later today. They will know to circle this place, and you will gain nothing by trying to locate them or lying in wait for them. But you will see to it that they, too, reach the boat unmolested."

"That's a tall order," Bolan said.

"That is all," Hu said. "My terms are fair, are they not?"

"Actually, no," Bolan said. "You're asking a lot for someone with nothing but a knife and an attitude."

The woman's eyes narrowed. "I have these men, as well, Cooper. I am not alone in—"

She was talking, and Bolan had his moment. His left hand snapped to the butt of the Beretta in the back of his waistband, where she wouldn't be watching for weapons. The gun came up and fired once, then twice. The two men flanking Hu were falling, bullet holes between their eyes, and Hu was screaming, knocking Baldero over, shoving him in front of her as his chair toppled. She scrambled over the cryptographer, stomping him in the head as she went, and launched herself at Bolan like a thrown cat, knocking the Beretta out of his hand.

Suddenly the knife blade was everywhere. Bolan felt it cut, and cut deeply, digging furrows from his arms and shoulders as he tried to fend her off and block the worst of the strikes. The leather shoulder holster holding the Tokarev fell away, and he realized she had been aiming for the straps of the harness with her first cuts. Then as he drew the Desert Eagle from his waistband a slash to his forearm caused him to drop the weapon. She had disarmed him in the hope of killing him at her leisure.

Bolan punched her in the jaw.

It was a glancing blow and didn't have much power behind it, but it dislodged her. Bolan backed off, through the adjoining door, into the curio shop. There was room to work, here. He drew the only weapon he had left—Kissinger's rosewood handle boot knife. The double-edged blade caught the light and glinted.

Hu snarled. A broad smile split her features. She was in her element, or so she thought. This was a woman who loved the blade and believed she was going to make short work of the big American who had dared intrude on her territory.

They circled each other for a few moments, Hu gauging the distance and taking his measure, or so she thought. Bolan kept the knife in front of him, his wrist locked, his arm stiff, as if trying to ward off evil with it. Hu made pass after pass, the knife coming ever closer, and she got more flashy as she went. She thought she had it in the bag—she thought Bolan was as good as carved up. She was going to make this a knife fight to remember, perhaps to recount to friends or lovers, Bolan thought. He could see her picturing it, could see her thinking about her victory as if it was already hers.

She started performing an elaborate routine with her blade,

either to impress him or simply to show off her abilities for whatever audience was available. The display was lost on Baldero, who was lying insensate on the floor of the adjoining room.

Hu's knife spun on the ring built into its handle, coming to full extension, snapping back, spinning completely around. The pattern was almost hypnotic, and it was meant to be. At any time, if she wished, she could move in with a goring, vicious slash or a hooking thrust that would disembowel her enemy. That was what she counted on. That was a technique she had doubtless used before.

That was what had happened to Rosen.

Bolan watched her face. When he judged that she was sufficiently lost in her fantasy of how she would celebrate her victory over him, he struck.

As Hu's knife sketched an arc before her body, Bolan turned his knife over, pointing it downward, and brought his free hand across his body. The two limbs imitated a scissors motion before him. His hand slapped Hu's forearm, and the blade of the inverted knife drew across the inside of her knife wrist. Bolan stepped to his left as he did it, moving at a forty-five-degree angle, closing in.

The woman screamed as she felt Bolan's keen blade slice into her flesh. He did not stop there. Hu, the knife fighter, was about to experience a knife fighter's fate. He drew the blade of his knife down across the outside of her forearm as he checked her with his free hand, then drove the stiffened fingers of his left hand into the back of her neck. He turned her body, using his knee up under the small of her back to shove her forward. Then, having slashed her, turned her, and driven the breath out of her, he bored into her, shoving her to the ground with the point of his knee and the back of his arm.

He could have put the knife into her as she went down, but she was unarmed and, for the moment, of no threat. At least, that was his assessment—until she hit the ground and, still screaming against the pain in her wrist, which pumped blood freely, rolled over onto her back. The little .25 automatic pistol that appeared in her fist had been in a sheath strapped to her ankle. It popped once, then twice, the rounds burning past Bolan and striking the wall of the curio shop. He threw himself back, knowing that one of the little rounds was going to find him, bracing himself to fight through the pain. He would have to push through, hoping the little bullets did not find something vital like an eye or his heart, and stab her to death while fighting for control of the weapon arm—

The burst of suppressed Type 85 gunfire was surprisingly loud. A line of ragged, bloody bullet holes erupted across her chest, traveled across the floor, punched a ladder up the wall and finally hit a light fixture in the ceiling, causing it to explode in a shower of glass and porcelain. Bolan ducked his head as he was showered with debris.

He turned, knife ready. He could throw the well-balanced blade if absolutely necessary, though that would be a tactic of absolute desperation.

He needn't have worried.

Baldero, his hands still bound together, held one of the Type 85 submachine guns awkwardly in both fists. He had either managed to bring the weapon under control or, more likely, he had sprayed out the entire magazine.

"Hey, Cooper," he said, blowing air through puffed out cheeks in a gesture of exhaustion. "Nice of you to finally show up."

"You took your time yourself."

"Yeah. Had kind of a concussion thing going on, or near like it."

"Join the club," Bolan said.

Baldero's face split into a wide grin. Bolan, despite himself, did the same.

The soldier wiped his knife on Hu's pant leg, then he used it to cut the tape binding Baldero's wrists.

"Freaking hard-core, man. Hard-core," Baldero said.

"You keep using that word," Bolan said.

"Well?" Baldero asked. "What would you call it?"

"I'd call it my job."

They recovered Bolan's weapons and equipment, and the Executioner replenished the war bag with a pair of Tokarev pistols and spare ammunition for them. He tucked the Beretta in his waistband opposite the Desert Eagle, as the shoulder holster was irreparable. Then he dialed the Farm, told them to give the local authorities the all-clear, and confirmed what he had learned from Hu.

"You're going to need a cleanup team in here," he told her.

"They're still working overtime to clean up the other messes you've made, Striker," Price teased, some of the tension easing from her voice now that Bolan had confirmed his reacquisition of Baldero. "Hal's gone through an entire bottle of antacids and almost smoked a cigar in the past few hours, he says."

"Tell him I'm sorry," Bolan said, "and that he's free to chew me out when next I see him."

"That won't be long," Price said. "He'll be waiting for you at the computer center. He's been there for the past hour."

"He was that confident I'd come through?"

"When have you not?"

Bolan said nothing to that. He grinned, causing Baldero to wonder about the side of the conversation he could not hear. "All right, Barb. Tell him to put out the welcome mat. We're coming in. And get some field patrols out here to augment the locals. This woman, Hu, indicated there would be other North Korean agents lurking about. If I'm picturing the map right, it would square with splitting their force so that these mysterious comrades could make a side trip to D.C."

"To deal with Tatro."

"I think so, yeah."

"All right, Striker. We're on it."

Bolan shepherded Baldero out of the shop and onto the street. They walked down the line of parked cars. Baldero suddenly stopped and started to shake. He looked pale.

"Whoa," Bolan said, taking him by the shoulder. "It's all right. Ride it out. Take deep breaths. In through your mouth, out through your nose. Slowly." He forced Baldero to do the deep breathing routine several times. The shakes started to subside.

"Is it…always like that when you do it?"

"No," Bolan said. "Not anymore."

"I never…I never killed anyone before," Baldero said. "Even a murderer…murderess…whatever. Even somebody like that. It's kind of freaking me out, man."

"Come on. We're almost there. We're going to drive into D.C., and that will be the end of this ride."

"'What a long, strange trip it's been,'" Baldero quoted. Bolan led them to the Tahoe and Baldero took in the blown-out front and rear glass, as well as the scorched rear seats. "Uh, Cooper?"

"Yeah."

"I think the backseat's on fire, man."

"Not anymore. I suppose it was."

Baldero slumped into the passenger seat and looked sick.

"It's all right," Bolan said. "It gets easier."

"I hope I don't find out."

"I hope you don't, either," Bolan said.

The Justice Department computer center was an unmarked building on a curiously lonely side street in the congested district of Washington, D.C. Once inside the outer lobby, which looked from the street like the entrance to any of the offices of countless nondescript bureaucratic functionaries, the armed guards and double-sealed steel security doors were enough to impress on a visitor that this was no ordinary facility. Those organizations operating with its sanction or under its umbrella worked hard to keep it a secret. There weren't many figures within government who knew of its exact address—or the full scope of its duties. A handful of men and women at the Pentagon, within the Department of Homeland Security, at Justice and sprinkled throughout other high-security departments, knew of it. Bolan supposed that the number added up to a significant one, when you took it in total.

The Executioner was more than a little concerned about the possibility of this Jim Tatro with DHS knowing about it.

He had conferred with the Farm several times during the drive from Alexandria, and this had been one of the questions he'd asked. Did Tatro give any indication that he knew of the computer center, or that Baldero would be transported there?

Price, through Kurtzman, had confirmed that no record of such a thing existed in Tatro's computer, but that meant very little. So much had transpired so quickly, in Bolan's whirlwind drive across Virginia, that Tatro could well have put two and two together and then discovered this destination. That he knew the facility was there was a distinct possibility.

Brognola had been waiting for them at the center. He had greeted Baldero cautiously but not with hostility. The cryptographer, for his part, could not stop singing Bolan's praises, assuming, perhaps reasonably if not correctly, that the big Fed was Bolan's boss and that a glowing account of Bolan's exploits would serve the soldier well in his continued employment. The Executioner had to admit that Baldero's heart was in the right place, as a somewhat flustered Brognola finally told Baldero that there would be time to debrief him later.

Bolan shook Brognola's hand, and the big Fed returned his strong grip. "You," he told the Executioner, "have been making my life pretty damned difficult these past few hours."

"I just do what I do," Bolan said.

"I know, and I'm grateful for it," Brognola said, "although my department's budget has been lowered to the tune of several official vehicles, thanks to your endangerment of municipal property. To say nothing of some vacant real estate that seems to have suffered severe structural damage, the result of, reports say, some very, very persistent vandals."

"Vandals. Right. Well, that sort of thing happens." Bolan nodded. "Add it to my tab."

"I'll do that," Brognola said. "As soon as they invent a number that big." More seriously, he said, "Did you have a lot of trouble?"

"Do you have time for a list?" Bolan said. "It doesn't matter. But Barb and her team are going to have their work cut out for them. This is a mess, Hal. We had, I don't know how many armed foreign nationals, some of them following others in a wagon train of terrorism across the state. They got in, they stayed in, and they wreaked havoc. It's only good luck that Baldero managed to stay ahead of them. Had they killed him, we'd all be in the thick of it."

"Don't think I don't know it." Brognola lowered his voice so Baldero, who was being wanded by the security staff at the entrance, could not hear. "The Man extends his thanks," he said. "I got word just before you arrived. We'll clean up the rest readily enough. You did good work, Striker, and on short notice. Thank you."

"If you want to thank me," Bolan said, "then cut the kid a break. I don't think he ever intended for this thing to get out, not like it did. It wasn't the smartest move, but he's no traitor. I'd hate to see him thrown down a hole and forgotten."

"I'll see to it," Brognola said. "I imagine your recommendation will carry a lot of weight with the boss."

"Aren't you the boss?"

"That's why it matters," Brognola said with a slight smirk. "All right, Striker. Get some rest. I'll be in touch after we debrief."

The guards ushered the cryptographer past the double security doors, but not before Baldero stopped them and extended his hand to Bolan.

"Agent Cooper," he said, "you saved my life. I want to thank you."

"I'd say you returned the favor," Bolan said. "In spirit at the very least. You've got a lot of strength, Daniel. Don't waste it. Put it to good use, for your country."

"I will," Baldero said. He made a face. "Damn, but you're a Boy Scout to the end."

Bolan said nothing. Baldero laughed, tossing him an abbreviated salute, and then he was being guided past the doors by Brognola. The doors sealed behind him.

Bolan shook his head. He thought that he would miss the younger man.

But not anytime soon.

He was turning for the glass doors leading out of the facility when he heard the roar of an engine. Suddenly, it was no longer a possibility that Tatro could have revealed the location of the computer facility.

It was a certainty.

The glass doors were torn from the hinges and shattered into tiny pieces. The taxicab that burst through was occupied by a single Asian man. He was pointing a Type 85 submachine gun out the window of the car.

Bolan had time to turn before the car hit him.

The Executioner hit the floor and rolled, pain washing over him and almost overwhelming him.

The Asian man opened fire. The stream of bullets traveled across the front desk and killed the receptionist sitting there. The armed guards responded with their service pistols, but the Asian cut them down until the magazine was empty. He climbed out of the car, tossing aside the now useless weapon, and rounded on Bolan.

"You!" he screamed.

Bolan looked up and saw the big man stalking him. He started to draw his weapon, but the Asian was on him, dragging him up and shaking him, then throwing him onto the hood of the taxicab. Bolan could feel the vibration of the brutalized engine racing; apparently its driver had left it in Neutral.

He tried to rise, but he was grabbed by the head and dragged from the hood of the car, then slammed onto the floor with bone-jarring force. The Asian's face loomed over his.

"I had hoped to find you here, murderer!" he roared. "Bloodthirsty swine! You make my work of vengeance easy, for I would have fought my way through all the ranks of your idiot men and slut women, if only to find you and squeeze the life from you!"

The Korean wrapped his hands around the soldier's throat and started squeezing. "I," he said, "am Kim Dae-Jung! You have offended the Democratic People's Republic of Korea! You have committed crimes against the leader! And you have killed my woman! You miserable beast, I shall beat you until you die!"

Bolan went for the knife and managed to get it out, but the Korean used one beefy hand to grab his adversary's wrist. He applied some sort of wristlock and Bolan was forced to release the blade. Only his own countermove, twisting free through the gap at Kim's thumb, saved his wrist from being broken.

There was nothing in Kim's eyes but animal hate and red-rimmed madness. Bolan felt himself picked up bodily and thrown through the air. He tried again for his guns, but they had been lost—his Kydex holster was empty and the Beretta was no longer in his waistband. He'd either lost them when he was hit by the car, or Kim had plucked them free.

He felt the cold fury in him, then, the levelheaded, righteous anger that fueled his crusade for justice and had kept him alive against countless predators. Shaking his head to clear it, he brought his hands up and squared off with the big Korean, who seemed intent on using his bare hands to murder his enemy.

"She died badly," Bolan taunted, hoping to send Kim over the edge. "She gave you up at the end, Kim. Told us everything we needed to know."

The man screamed, deep in his throat. He launched a furious attack, his skills obviously based in Korea's Tae Kwon Do. This was not the point-fighting martial art taught in strip malls across America, a popular pastime of children. This was the original, brutal, full-contact Tae Kwon Do only rarely found outside the Koreas, and it was a system devoted to hurting and killing.

Kim's kicks were high and long. He had no trouble keeping his balance, and the more he fought the more deadly calm he seemed to become. As he punched, kicked and danced around Bolan, each man fighting for a better position from which to best his adversary, he seemed to lose the unfocused rage that had driven him. Instead, he became…centered, was the word that came to Bolan's mind, as he used his footwork and his arms and legs to slip, dodge and block the Korean's attacks.

They could not keep facing off forever. Sooner or later, one of them would tire. Kim was fresh, or relatively so. Bolan was battered from countless firefights and felt as if he had at least a cracked rib. It wasn't every day that an opponent opened personal combat with him by hitting him with a car. He was feeling the effects.

He had to take the psychological advantage, had to press, had to continue to attack. He had to overwhelm Kim, refuse to give him time to recoup or counter, if he was to take and keep the momentum in this battle for his life.

"Your leader," he said, "is a coward and a fool."

"I do not disagree," Kim said, smiling broadly, throwing a kick up past Bolan's head that the soldier only barely managed to avoid.

"Your woman was a whore," Bolan said. "She was indulging herself with your men when I found her and killed her."

That did it. What Kim did not feel for country, or political loyalty, he apparently felt strongly for Hu, a woman with whom it appeared he shared a bloody-minded madness that made them both unspeakable killers. Hu had been only too eager to use her knife, and he had seen her desire to cut him, to tear him, to stab him to death, in the depths of her half-mad eyes. That was why Ayalah Rosen had died as she did—and at the memory of the beautiful Israeli woman's tragic death, Bolan found his own anger rising, his own righteous fury driving him forward.

He planted a solid punch in Kim's midsection, doubling him over and taking his breath. Then he dropped Kim down on his knee, feeling the man's teeth clack together, the knee of his blacksuit pants coming away bloody. Another stomp drove the side of his boot into the Korean's shin and then down onto the man's ankle. Kim twisted away before Bolan could get the ankle break he had sought.

Kim began throwing kick after kick. Bolan planted a combat boot in his thigh, brutalizing the muscle there, and his opponent started limping on that leg. The Korean staggered forward, throwing a series of wild, hooking punches. The Executioner stepped in, stopped the punch inside at the shoulder and the forearm, and snaked his hand from Kim's shoulder up to the man's jawline. Throwing his adversary's captured arm up and over at the triceps, he dug his fingers into the Korean's neck and jaw, finding the nerve and squeezing with all his strength. Bolan twisted Kim's head.

The man screamed in pain. Bolan continued twisting and Kim gave in to physics and body mechanics, landing heavily on the floor. Bolan landed on him with his knees.

He drove one knee up into Kim's head and slammed the other down and under Kim's arm, until he had achieved a sitting position with the Korean's arm locked between his legs. Then he applied pressure, the man's arm snapping like a dry twig.

Bolan shifted, throwing the struggling, snarling, spitting, shrieking Korean's arm up and over his own throat. He applied pressure again, choking Kim with his own arm, ducking his head to the side when Kim tried to head butt him.

The Korean had played the ground game before and managed, against the sound of grating bones in his arm, to buck and twist out of position. Bolan let him roll over and then planted a knee in the back of his chest. Finally, he wrapped his arms in a sloppy headlock around Kim's head and neck. The Korean bucked again, and Bolan was thrown down and to the side, still with a death grip on his adversary's head.

The Korean's neck snapped, a sound like wet pine logs scraping across each other. He convulsed and went limp in Bolan's grasp.

The Executioner stood and looked down at the dead man.

Another predator, this one a mad dog, had just left this world for the next.

Epilogue

The opulent headquarters of Sirux-Gibbmann, in its little corner of the Ivory Coast, had proved relatively easy to penetrate. Bolan stood in an anteroom outside Sirus Wassermann's office, listening to Price on the other end of the line as he held his secure sat phone to his ear. Behind him, a string of dead mercenaries dotted the hallway, and on every level below this penthouse, the building was filled with corpses.

The Executioner had come calling.

"Local authorities found the body of a North Korean national, identified as Yoon Jin-Sang, stuffed into a mailbox outside Alexandria," Price was saying. "The North Koreans are denying any connection, but our sources say that Yoon was highly placed within their military and intelligence services."

"How did he die?" Bolan asked.

"He was beaten to death," Price said. "Also, strangled. And he had a bullet through his head. Not to mention being stuffed into the mailbox, of course. In short, whoever killed him, killed him a lot."

"They killed the hell out of him, I'd say." Bolan nodded to no one, the anteroom empty. With one exception, the soldier was the only living being in the Sirux-Gibbmann building at that moment.

"Some of our contacts at NSA are working on a theory," Price said. "They think Yoon was a handler. The one you killed in D.C., Kim Dae-Jung, was known to be a loose cannon, and there are rumors that he was disgraced in North Korea. We're not sure why, but it probably has to do with just how uncontrollable he was."

"So maybe Yoon, the handler, wanted to call it off or cut their losses," Bolan theorized. "Kim beats him, strangles him, shoots him and mails him postage due. And then, probably working on information Tatro revealed before *he* was hand-canceled, Kim turns kamikaze and comes for us at Baldero's destination, running out a suicide play for love, honor or anger. Something like that?"

"Looks that way," Price said. "How are your ribs feeling?"

"Taped up," Bolan said. "Not a problem."

"I'll be sure to look you over when you get back to the Farm," Price said. "I wouldn't want you to hurt yourself."

"I imagine that's probably wise," Bolan said warmly. Then, more briskly, he said, "I assume the other loose ends have been tied up?"

"Yes," Price said. "Tatro's 'business associates' have been ferreted out thanks to the data in his files. They'll be spending some time in prison. Probably all the time they'll ever have."

"Speaking of that," Bolan said, "did Baldero come out of this okay?"

"He did," Price confirmed. "He cut a deal through Hal and, at last count, he was hard at work on his decryption program. He's not without his prospects once that's done. Apparently NSA says they'd love to have him working for them. Offered him a nice, big salary. He said he'd think about it."

"Sounds like Daniel," Bolan said. "All right, Barb. Have Jack standing by to fly me out."

"You're done there?"

"Not yet," Bolan said, "but I will be."

"Okay, Striker. Fly safe. I'll look forward to seeing you when you get in."

"So will I, Barb," Bolan said. "So will I. Striker out."

He closed the phone.

Wielding the suppressor-equipped Beretta 93-R, Bolan switched the machine pistol to single shot. The metal doors before him were secured, but they were built for looks, not strength. Three kicks from his combat booted right foot were enough to bend the dead bolt out of shape. He pushed the doors open and stepped inside.

In the middle of a nest of computer equipment, Sirus Wassermann looked up. He swallowed hard as he discreetly reached for something under his desk. "Look," he said. "Whoever you are, I can pay you. I have a fortune at my disposal. We can cut a deal."

"No," the Executioner said, "we can't."

He put a single bullet between Wassermann's eyes, and the gun the man had retrieved dropped to the floor.

Now Bolan was done.

* * * * *